"It's a lovely cr

"It is," Simon agreed. "Last night, I took my niece and nephew out to the mountains. We saw a shooting star. You would have liked it, I think."

Olivia nodded thoughtfully. "I think so, yes. Your niece and nephew are very lucky to have you. I would have loved to have seen that shooting star. I've only ever seen one or two."

He chuckled, shaking his head. "They're fun children. Next time, I'll be sure to bring you."

The idea made her heart flutter. He sounded so sure of a next time, of a future. Olivia's gaze dropped. They were already nearly touching, and she could feel his warmth. He was so close. Swallowing, she tried to think of something to say. Wrinkling her nose, it took her a minute to consider her options.

"I would like that," she said at last, and looked over to find him watching her thoughtfully. He was already smiling, and she returned it willingly. "Very much," she added.

Annie Boone admits that sweet love stories are a passion. She also enjoys history, so writing about the two together is a perfect match. Adding spiritual elements reminds her of her own faith as she writes. Annie lives in Atlanta, Georgia, with her husband and the two most wonderful cats in the world. She loves to travel, cook for her family and friends, and watch as many sports as possible. Of course, she also loves to read.

COLORADO
MATCHMAKER
VOL. 2
ANNIE BOONE

FEATURING: Rowena and Jeb & Olivia and Simon

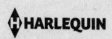

ISBN-13: 978-1-335-08024-0

Colorado Matchmaker Volume 2

Copyright © 2020 by Harlequin Books S.A.

Rowena and Jeb
First published in 2018 by Annie Boone. This edition published in 2020.
Copyright © 2018 by Annie Boone

Olivia and Simon
First published in 2018 by Annie Boone. This edition published in 2020.
Copyright © 2018 by Annie Boone

**Recycling programs
for this product may
not exist in your area.**

This edition published by arrangement with Harlequin Books S.A.

For questions and comments about the quality of this book,
please contact us at CustomerService@Harlequin.com.

Harlequin Enterprises ULC
22 Adelaide St. West, 40th Floor
Toronto, Ontario M5H 4E3, Canada
www.Harlequin.com

Printed in U.S.A.

CONTENTS

ROWENA AND JEB

Chapter One

New York City; 1880

The great grandfather clock struck midnight, and chimed loudly in the main hall. Twelve chimes that seemed to shake the floor and still made Rowena jump every time the first clang pealed out. *Well, not every time*, she admitted to herself, but it happened every time she was actually in the room. Rubbing an eye, the young woman tried to shrink back into the shadows to pull herself together.

After clearing up her vision, Rowena tied her hair back. It was most likely that soon it would be untied by someone not of her liking, but she did it anyway. She knew it made her look five years younger, and hoped that would convince everyone to ignore her. Clear eyes, hair out of the face, and then she tried to pull her skirt down lower. It was just shy of the tops of her boots, and it was a chilly evening.

"It's too cold for this nonsense," she muttered to herself, in the vain hope it would suddenly double in length.

It was a fabric like a cheap silk that shined in the light, but was flimsy and prone to stains and tears. As she bent over, a thick strand of her long brown hair escaped the braid and she groaned.

"Hiding in the corner again?" Gertrude walked by, holding her tray high. "Come along, my little squirrel. We've all got jobs to do."

The younger woman pursed her lips at the silly nickname and watched the tall blonde stroll away down into the hall. This was where the fancy parlor with the grand clock and the well-lit lanterns were. But further into the saloon were low lights, no concept of time, and too much of everything Rowena hated.

A few minutes later, she could avoid it no longer. Already she was starting to get noticed and could feel the eyes on her. At least, the girl knew, they wouldn't be able to see her well under the low lights. Swallowing, she reached the ballroom and raised her tray higher in the air.

"There you are, little lady," Mr. Sylvester Pyrion chuckled as she passed his roulette table. "I was wondering where you've been. You haven't been avoiding me, have you?" Slouched over the counter, the candles lit the grease in his hair and in his smile. The buttons on his shirt were near bursting as though they wanted to be far away from here and she knew exactly how they felt.

"Not at all, sir." With a tight smile, she obediently shared her tray with him, and he switched his glass for fresh champagne. But as Rowena attempted to step away, his hand slipped over hers and the tray wobbled. "Oh! I—oh, my!"

The others laughed around the table, watching her

as though she were more interesting than the cards in their hands. Gritting her teeth, she pulled away harder this time but not before the straying fingers reached her hips. Rowena jumped and turned, scampering off to the sound of their guffaws.

"And they all wear wedding rings," she shuddered.

After two more turns around the room and spending most of the time escaping wandering hands, Rowena needed to catch her breath. Coughing from all the cigar smoke hovering in the room, she found one of the parlors empty and slipped in as she rubbed her watery eyes.

There was no clock here, but it certainly had to be past two in the morning, a time when everyone should be sleeping. Having been working in the ballroom for a year now, Rowena was still not used to being awake at this time. Just as she was considering hiding out here for the rest of the evening, the curtain opened.

"I'm sorry—" She stopped abruptly when she saw the look on Mr. Hiram Beal's face. The wicked grin on his face faded into a grim expression and the girl behind him, Gertrude's sister Mary Anne, tittered shyly. Her red lip stain was smeared, and her eyes were bright and unfocused. The aroma of cheap cologne hung heavily in the air, not much better than the smoke and whiskey. Rowena's cheeks heated up and her eyes skirted down. "I'll go."

But he stood in her way, unmoving. It was a small parlor, round with only a slim entrance with a curtain hung over it, obviously meant for private moments. It made Rowena feel sick to her stomach but there wasn't much room in a gambling house like this. "No. She will go."

Mr. Beal released Mary Anne, pushing her away harshly. The girl stumbled into the hazy smoke and Rowena's throat closed up as she found herself alone with… What was he to her?

Her master? Owner? Simply her employer? For three years she had been trapped in this little gambling house, the scourge of the area. Ever since her uncle had lost her in a card game here, this had become her life. No matter how often she saw Mr. Beal, in daylight or candlelight, the queasiness never subsided.

"I need to…um, deliver more drinks," she stammered, and hurriedly turned back to her tray sitting on top of the cushions. "I just needed a breath of fresh air, I swear, I'm not being lazy."

"Not what? Being lazy, you say?" He crossed his arms and leisurely looked her over. It made her feel like a pig at market, and she wanted more than anything to push him away and run off. But she couldn't do something like that, not when she didn't know what would happen next. "Rowena, isn't it?"

"Yes, sir?"

It was as though he were sucking the life out of her with that dark hooded stare. She shifted, trying again to pull her skirt down. "You've grown," the man said finally, his dark eyes considering her. She knew he was at least in his fifties. He dyed his hair and his mustache black every week, the ink a wobbly ridge against his receding hairline. He smelled a bit like a dead animal, and she was glad she hadn't eaten in several hours. "You've been here for what, five years?"

She shook her head and fiddled with the tray. "Three.

Three years. Two were spent cleaning, and now I'm serving in the main social room."

He licked his lips. "You were such a scrawny little thing, when you arrived. But I certainly got my money's worth now that you're all grown up."

Rowena couldn't take it any longer. Holding the tray now with both hands in front of her, she tried to step around him. "I need to get back out there, sir, I'm working, you know."

"Don't concern yourself with that," he waved a hand in the air, and started to drape it over her shoulder. This action, however, meant that he had stepped aside and the way out was clear. Her heart skipped a beat at the opening. "Relax here with me. Just for a bit."

His sweat soaked shirt brushed against her bare arm and she felt another wave of nausea. Hurriedly she slid forward, and through the curtain. "Sorry, sir," she murmured and escaped the room. The thought of being alone with him any longer than a few seconds was too much to bear.

Refusing to look back, Rowena walked stiffly across the room and out the door. There would be no fresh air in a place like this, not a moment's respite. Though the evening was only half over, Rowena decided she wasn't needed anymore. She would deal with any punishment later in the bright light of day.

Dropping her tray in the front room, she slipped out a back door and made her way towards the barn. Tugging at her clothes along the way, she picked up a cloak by the barn that one of the girls had left behind and made her way up the side stairs.

In the attic, there were empty beds and cots everywhere since the other girls were still working. Rowena stumbled over to her bed, changed out of her work dress, and slipped beneath her blankets. Only then did the shivering stop, knowing she was safe now, and alone. Just the way she liked it.

Chapter Two

Rocky Ridge, Colorado; 1880

"Easy, now," Lucas's hands slipped around Susannah's waist as he eased her off the horse. Only once both feet were on the ground did she let out her breath. He gave her a look upon hearing it, but they both knew it was an old habit. "You'd think after years of riding her she'd be more…"

Distracting him, she ran a finger across the buttons on his shirt. "She's the sweetest thing, Lucas. But some habits die very, very hard. Now, would you be so kind as to help me with the saddle?" She offered him a smile and her husband complied without resistance. Together, they lifted the saddle and brushed their horses down before heading towards their house.

The sun was setting behind the mountains, leaving the sky streaked in a stream of beautifully warm colors. Susannah sighed, linking fingers with her husband. It was something she never tired of, having such good company in a lovely place like this. Such a moment was nearly perfect. Nearly.

Absently her fingers drifted over her stomach, and Lucas stopped humming when he noticed. The scar on his face tightened as he slowed their pace and reached the porch. "Susie?"

She dropped her hand and turned with a forced smile. His gaze drifted back up to her face, looking at her in wary concern. "I was just admiring the sunset. It's lovely, isn't it?" But after nine years of marriage, there was no chance of her lying to him. They knew each other too well. The man waited for her as she sighed and shrugged. "It's just so empty, Lucas. A big house, and no one to fill it."

He guided her through the door into the warmth. Winter was fading away but the evenings were still cool. Lucas wrapped a shawl over her shoulders and she followed him to the fireplace, bringing the embers back to life. "We still have our stragglers," he reminded her.

She smiled at the name. It wasn't very kind, but it was a joke of theirs. With such a large home, and with him in town so often working as the Rocky Ridge sheriff, it was normal for him to return with the occasional weary traveler when the town's hotel was booked full. In fact, that morning before church they had dropped off a family of four at the train station so they could continue west. A darling family, with energetic twin boys. They'd had blonde hair and brown eyes, just like she'd imagined their own children would have looked like.

For a minute her thoughts drifted, trying once again to imagine what it would be like to have their house filled with the children they had dreamed of. Having been raised in a small home in Boston, she had only been able to imagine having perhaps two children. But out here in the west, why, some folks had even ten little ones running around. She couldn't imagine that many, but something in between would have been nice for them.

Many days in town, Lucas could be found playing with the children and she knew he would have liked all the little bustling feet and loud laughter within their own home. It bore down on her, that happy dream that couldn't happen.

The spark of a flame drew her forth and Susannah joined Lucas closer on the hearth, pulling out the poker so he wouldn't hurt himself. Just last month he'd nearly lost his hand trying to move a log without using the iron. His thumb was still bandaged, and slowly healing. "We do have our stragglers," she echoed after a moment, and then looked at him hesitantly. "But I still think we could…well, we could have more folks here."

He raised his eyebrow. "And what, turn this into a hotel? It's a little far from town, darling." But after a moment, the tall man remembered what they had discussed in pieces and parts over the last few years. Lucas sighed heavily. "No, not that again. We don't need more mouths to feed, and strangers walking in and out every day."

"They wouldn't just be any type of stranger," she hurriedly corrected him. "Girls, young women who wanted to come here. And they wouldn't just be taking things from us. They could pay, room and board and earn their keep. After all, they'd need to learn how to live here and farm. I've been thinking it all through, honestly." She looked at him expectantly, hoping he would soften just a bit.

Lucas remained silent and raised an eyebrow. He was almost able to hide the scowl as she continued.

"We have the rooms, and could build more as necessary. With them helping with the farming and the cooking, there's plenty of help to make sure we have the food we need. They'll bring their own clothes and I have plenty of sewing tools. I can teach them laundry, and you can teach them about…oh I don't know, horses? And then," she hesitated, and Lucas broke in.

She didn't like the expression on his face, the consternation mixed with pity. "And then what? I don't know if we really have the time for this, to take on so much."

Though she knew he was concerned about her idea, something forced Susannah to push on, hoping he would really listen. Taking his hand, she caught his expression. "Take on so much what? Lucas, we have plenty of time and you know it. I can't just keep doing this, pretending nothing is—" she cut herself off to take a deep breath before forging on. "I want to be helping others if I have the time to spare. We're Christian people, aren't we?" She waited to see if he at least agreed with her logic.

He frowned again, but nodded curtly.

Susannah smiled hopefully then wrinkled her nose. "Why, just think of it. What if I'd had a place to go when I first arrived here?" she pointed out, trying to bring out his kindness. "I wouldn't have been bothered by that man and I wouldn't have been alone. And I hate to say it, but it definitely took a long time for me to learn how to farm and especially to ride a horse. What if I could help other women learn to do all the things that were troublesome for me at the start?"

For a moment he just looked at her, slowly thinking it through. It was hard to read his expression now, and Susannah waited. Her heart pounded in her chest, wondering what he was thinking and what he would eventually say. "A boarding house for young women," he said at last. "That's what you really want?"

Opening her mouth to respond, she paused and considered this. After all, he appeared to be really considering her idea and she had to respect that. They didn't joke about things like this, and Lucas took his decisions very seriously. "Yes," Susannah nodded at last. "I think it would be nice for me—for us, I mean—to have people here more often."

"How often are we talking?" He asked her carefully, glancing away now to add more logs to the fire. A small beat of her heart skipped, knowing he was now working out how this might work out for them.

Brightening, she scooted closer so their hips were touching, and she left an arm draped over his. "A few at a time, I'm sure. I don't know how long they would stay. A few weeks, perhaps? Possibly longer for some. And I'd be wanting to set them up with the men, of course, but they'd have to be good ones, you know. The really good men. Mostly from here. I know there are plenty of bachelors in Rocky Ridge, after all," she added. "And why, I think that even—"

His hand grabbed hers. It was dirty from the wood, but it was warm. "Are you saying you want to play matchmaker, too?" He raised an eyebrow at her and she saw the twinkle in his eye.

"Why not?" She pouted. "It worked with Eleanor."

"Yes, but it doesn't mean that it will work every time," he articulated carefully. "And that's a lot more responsibility than just running a boarding house."

She offered him a sheepish smile. "Well, I've always been up for a challenge." But he just sighed and wrapped an arm around her as they stood up and went over to the couch to relax.

Wrapped in his embrace, Susannah brushed her hair away from her shoulder and listened to his heartbeat. Lucas didn't need to say anything more to let her know that he was considering it. This meant she was getting to him, and hopefully in a little more time the man might oblige. But she wouldn't push it now, she decided, and would give it some time. He wasn't convinced, but she was determined to show him it would be worth their time, just as soon as he told her yes.

Chapter Three

New York City; 1880

"Do wear it," Gertrude teased her, waving the small golden tin in front of her face. "You'd be the belle of the ball. Or do you think you're too good for it?" There was an underlying nastiness in the tone, and it set Rowena on edge.

Shying away from the lip stain, she shook her head and started towards the stairs. "I'm not, you know that. I don't want anyone looking at me or—"

"Or touching you," Mary Anne finished for her in a phony tone. "You say it every night, but we have such a hard time believing you. Why, I had two men nearly putty in my hands last week. But then you showed up, and they forgot all about me. I could have made ten whole dollars if you hadn't been in the way!"

The other three girls laughed, throwing their heads back and making their big earrings jingle. Uncomfortable, Rowena continued slinking towards the door. "No, really. I promise, I'll try harder to stay away. I keep telling them no, but they don't listen. It's not my fault."

"You're just teasing them," Louella scowled. "As if telling them you're not interested would make them ignore you. It's like you're dangling sweets in front of a child. Even you can't be that innocent."

She ran out the door before she could hear anything else. Some days were fine between the girls, but then there were nights like these where they just couldn't get along. Shaking her head, Rowena wrapped herself in her shawl and once at the bottom of the steps, leaned against the old barn and had a moment for herself.

It didn't make sense, and though she was old enough to know the ways of flirtation and womanhood at twenty, Rowena shied away from it. The world of lust and dark shadows held no interest for her, and the men she saw every night left her shuddering and disgusted. But why was it that she could say yes or no and it would mean the same thing to men? It just made no sense, and only invited others to mock her.

She hated it that she was here, immersed in this world. She only had a little time longer and then she'd be on her own. Yes, soon she would be allowed to leave.

The twins made their way down, whispering and passing her glances as they walked past and pretended to ignore her. Rowena didn't mind, and preferred it when people left her alone. She tugged at her hair, trying to use it to shield her face so they wouldn't see her.

"You're going to be late," Eliza called out. "And you know Antony doesn't like that."

"Antony doesn't like anything," Rowena scowled, but obeyed all the same. Leaving her shawl by the doors, she tried to adjust her clothes and trailed after the women. They checked in with Antony who scowled at each and every one of them, and then sent them on their way with trays to deliver drinks to the thirsty patrons.

There was music playing in the main room, which livened things up. It also gave Rowena something more to focus on. The noise was oddly soothing, something that she could rely upon. She would take any distraction she could from a place like this.

"Psst," Gertrude nudged her as she passed. "Beal is looking for you."

Frowning, she glanced back at the woman already walking away. "What?"

But the older girl just shot her a look before strutting off, strutting in high heels and such a small petticoat. Tossing her long curls over her shoulders, her frown slipped off as she found her next target. Rowena watched Gertrude slip onto the man's lap and wrap an arm around his neck to whisper something in his ear. He grinned, and shot the girl a look that made Rowena turn away in a hurry.

Scenes like that, they just weren't easy to get used to. Once again, she couldn't believe she'd been plunked down into the middle of this filthy world. It wasn't who she was and it wasn't what she wanted for her life.

Suddenly she remembered. Mr. Beal was looking for her? He hadn't spoken to her in weeks, though he certainly watched her close enough. His gaze made her feel as though ants were crawling over every inch of her skin. Over the last year, the man's interest in her had only grown and that made her nervous. Because she knew what it was, that look in his eyes. Rowena could recall this happening to most of the other girls, the ones who had giggled and submitted with the hopes of securing their future. Rowena didn't know what else to do but keep her head down, and prayed he forgot her.

As Rowena made her rounds, she kept an eye out for the empty glasses, quietly trading them for fresh, full ones before she could be noticed. It was a tricky art but she'd had enough practice to now frequently escape unscathed.

Just as the evening was coming to an end, she was preparing to turn in early. Tips were split between all the employees, but over the last year or so they had stopped including her as the women claimed that she kept ruining their chances with the customers. They even claimed she was earning enough on her own, though she wasn't doing what they thought that she was doing. Such a thought made her shudder, and she turned to slip out the door.

"And where might you be going?" An arm slipped over her bare shoulder, a sweaty palm gripping tightly. She knew the voice before she even turned, gritting her teeth as she tried to politely smile. Mr. Hiram Beal was there, a wicked sneer poised just below his crooked nose.

Feigning innocence, she ducked her face behind her hair. "I was searching for more empty mugs. Someone was asking me for…for, um, one." He glanced at her tray with three perfectly fine and full mugs of ale. "A different one," she tried to add.

"If I didn't know better," Beal hummed with a slight slur, "I might think you've been avoiding me? Eh?" His grip tightened again and he pulled her a little closer to him.

She stumbled off balance, nearly falling into him. The tray tilted, and the full mugs fell over before she could collect them all. They crashed and spilled over his shoes, but he shrugged it off, his eyes still focused on her face. "You've turned into a right pretty thing. Have I told you that?"

Her throat constricted, and Rowena felt the hair on the back of her neck stand up. Trying to remain calm, she looked for an escape. "That's right kindly of you, sir. But really, I should get back to work. It's getting late, after all."

"Hey, I own you." He frowned. "Don't talk back to me. Do not disrespect me."

"Sir, I just work here to pay off the debt," she fought for the courage she so firmly believed she had somewhere inside. That belief got her though the days and especially through the nights. From what her uncle had told her, she only had another year left to pay the fines. She knew she could manage just another year. After that, she'd be free to go wherever she wished.

Not back home of course, she didn't want that. Her whiskey-soaked relatives wouldn't care either way, and that's why she was here in the first place. Somewhere new, and somewhere safe. That's all she wanted, and she just needed a year to get there. So Rowena swallowed her fear, and glanced down at the mess of broken glass and spilled ale on the already sticky floor.

"Oh!" She exclaimed. "I should clean that up. I need to go."

Usually this was enough to distract anyone who de-

tained her and allow for an escape, but it took an unexpected turn this time. Before she knew it, Beal had
pushed her against the wall, his hand was wrapped
around her throat. The shove knocked the breath out
of her and she gasped for air, eyes wide.

"You can't play these games with me," he hissed.
"I know what you are. You act so coy, but you are just
one of them. Why, I bet you've been hiding in all those
parlors with the other men who come in here. They certainly talk about you enough." His free hand slipped to
her knee, and started to trail upwards, brushing against
the skirt.

Wiggling, she tried to move his arms away, clawing
at the one on her leg and trying to slide out of his grasp.
"No, you have it all wrong. I don't do that. I'd never do
that! Please stop!"

"Stop!" The sound shocked her so much that she
froze, closing her eyes to try to regain her composure.
She could feel him there, pressing himself against her.
Though others passed in the hallway, Rowena knew no
one would care to do anything about this. "I own you.
Never forget that," he hissed in her ear.

She tried to turn away. "No, I only work here. I'm
just paying off my uncle's debt until—"

To her surprise, he stepped away and threw his head
back in laughter. The movement surprised her so much
that she didn't know what to do.

"Is that what he said?" Mr. Beal laughed so hard that
he choked and started to wheeze, doubling over to catch
his breath. Rowena couldn't decide if she should run or
help him. "You dimwitted fool. No, he sold you to me.
This isn't something you can pay off, girl. You're here,

and you're mine. And there's nothing you can do about it." He paused and gave her a sneer as he looked down at the mess on the floor. "Now I'm going to give you two minutes to clean up this mess, and then I want to see you in that parlor!" He pointed to the nearest curtain, and gave her a dark look.

Unable to help herself, Rowena obeyed. Bending down, she shakily picked up the broken glass, putting it on the shabby tray and running everything to the kitchens. They took care of the glass and she wiped off the tray. Her heart pounded as she looked towards the swinging doors, knowing what the second set of orders meant.

A knot formed inside her belly, threatening to take control. It made her sick. Trying to breathe, an idea came to her quickly enough that she grasped immediately, and didn't think about it twice. If there was no debt, a small voice inside her reasoned, then she might be stuck there forever.

If she wasn't willing to accept a future of forever in this place, it was better to act sooner rather than later. And that meant now. Slipping through the back door, Rowena knew she only had a few minutes before Mr. Beal knew something was amiss.

"Whoa!" Mary Anne hollered as Rowena darted around her in the hall. "Watch it, Squirrel!" She put out a hand to swipe at her, but the young girl dodged the half-hearted blow and made it out the door.

"Hurry, hurry," she murmured, looking around before running up to the barn's attic. Trying to move quietly, Rowena changed out of her clothes and grabbed the bundle she kept trapped beneath a floorboard. It was the money she had been saving up, along with a few baubles she had collected over the years.

In and out in under a minute, Rowena darted down the stairs and around the building. Clutching her few belongings, she looked around carefully and glanced back to see if anyone was following. Soon she was on the main road and though she was frightened, she just kept running. She had no idea where to go in the city, but surely anything was better than there. It had to be.

Chapter Four

Rocky Ridge, Colorado; 1880

The house was cleaner than ever before, and that was saying something. At the bottom of the stairs, Susannah clasped her hands together and considered the view. The table had two more chairs, and they'd added to the pantry. There were more blankets near the fireplace along with much more yarn and plenty of needles.

She knew the lean-to against the barn was well stocked with flower pots and small shovels, just as the bookcase held plenty of books and writing utensils. The Jessups were very fortunate, especially without needing to have spent money on others for a long time. But that, Susannah thought hopefully, was about to change.

It had been over a month since she had placed her advert. Promising room and board for a small fee, it was directed to single women back East who sought shelter and a better future. Knowing there had to be more ladies like herself and her friend Eleanor who desired to leave the cities for something different, Susannah had high hopes of helping them with a fresh start.

There were high hopes, especially since no one had as yet replied to the ad.

"Susie, darling, I thought you were going to sleep in today? You were up so late." Lucas padded down quietly, wrapping an arm around her before she noticed he was there. The clever man, having spent enough years in the Ranger service, could creep around anywhere before she ever heard a thing. It was maddening, including that wicked grin of his that he wore whenever he did this to her.

Wrapping an arm around his waist, she allowed him to kiss her forehead. "I know, I'm sorry. I couldn't stay there any longer. The snow," she added for explanation when he raised an eyebrow. "It's only the snow. Besides, you weren't even doing anything interesting. You were starting to snore."

"I don't snore," he kissed her again. "Do you want to go outside then?"

After surveying the house one more time, Susannah nodded. She knew she needed to be patient, and to enjoy what she had. Rubbing his back, she was about to turn upstairs before she gasped. "Oh! I was going to make muffins. Should I do that first?"

He scratched his head thoughtfully, mussing his dark hair even more. "Whichever you prefer, I suppose."

Looking at him, she could tell his eyes were still dark with sleep. For a moment she frowned, trying to remember if it had been her fault. Once in bed, she had a tendency to grow restless and had a hard time sleeping throughout the night. But she couldn't remember moving around too much, and could have sworn she slept through most of it.

"Perhaps we could return to bed?" She decided after a moment and then grinned at him. Clasping his hand in hers, she picked up her skirt with the other hand and started pulling him back towards their bedroom. "It is just us, after all. We can do whatever we want."

"Yes, but the cows…"

Leaning over from a higher step, she kissed his cheek. "Don't worry, I think they're still asleep, too. Besides, neither of us are dressed for such cold weather. Come along and let's see to the cows a bit later." And they took their time, tumbling back into bed for just a while before they each dressed for the day.

Lucas left to tend to the animals, and she made breakfast. Muffins, eggs, bacon. All her husband's favorites. She set the table and decided to go help in the barn. Susannah pulled on her boots and coat before stepping outside. She shivered and pulled her thick knitted scarf tighter around her neck before starting through her husband's tracks through the snow.

And she was nearly there when a sudden force struck her shoulder, and knocked her off balance. With a screech, she fell face first into the snow and everything went cold. Shivering, she hurried up to her knees and squinted around.

Only then did she realize what had happened.

"You scoundrel!" Susannah shouted, climbing to her feet with a handful of snow between her mittens. Lucas offered a cheeky wave just in time for her own snowball to hit his neck. He jumped, spitting out the snow. His expression made her laugh, the snow falling out of her hair.

He started after her. Yelping, she tried to throw two more snowballs at him before he could reach her, but she missed both times. Futilely she attempted to run away, but suddenly his arms were wrapped around her waist, raising her off her feet. By then they were both laughing, even as she landed and fell back on him, both of them falling down into the snow.

"You took forever to come out here," he chuckled.

She gave him a look. "Oh, I'm terribly sorry to have inconvenienced your urge to throw something at me." Rolling her eyes, she let him laugh one more time before grabbing a handful of snow beside them and tossing it in his face.

He coughed through his laughter, and retaliated with a kiss. Lucas's chilled nose nudged her cheek, but his lips were warm and sent a delightful shiver down her spine. After all this time, he could still make her feel like a young bride. She permitted him one more kiss, before they scrambled up, now soaked to the skin.

"Let's find some dry clothes," she helped him to his feet breathlessly, "And then we've got breakfast waiting for us." Lucas wrapped an arm around her as they started inside, hungry and eager for warmth.

The following day, Susannah accompanied Lucas to town. He would stay there for a few hours, and enough work had been done around the house that Susannah could join him without guilt. She spent the morning running errands and then brought lunch. They were sitting at his desk when his deputy, Jeb Harbin, came through the door.

The tall man, dark-haired and modest, bowed his head in apology. Pulling off his hat, he offered a sheepish grin and started backwards. "Oh, I didn't know there was company. I apologize," and then he bumped into the wall. "Sorry to interrupt, Missus."

She shook her head. "Oh, don't be! No, come in. I thought I would annoy my husband for a little bit. You're more than welcome to join us, Mr. Harbin. Would you like a sandwich? There's plenty to go around."

A moment of hesitation was all that she needed to bring forward a chair and then she put a sandwich in the younger man's hands. There was something about the man that made Susannah want to wrap him in a blanket and set him by the fire with a nice bowl of soup. It worked well, since he had little experience around women and had no choice but to obey her now.

"Well, thanks," he offered. "That's mighty nice of you. I'm still living off tack and jerky most days."

Returning to Lucas's desk, Susannah frowned. "What? I thought you were settling down here, Mr. Harbin. Surely you've got a plot of land somewhere, with a cow or two? At least some chickens?" A thought dawned on her and she narrowed her eyes at the young man.

With his mouth full, Jeb shook his head. "Oh I have the land, all right. Lucas made sure of that. There's a nice small plot halfway to Colorado Springs. It's just on the edge of town, you see. But I'm still working on my house, and I don't even know what to do with animals. Horses are something I understand, but I've never even touched a chicken."

She furrowed her brow. "Mr. Harbin, I know so very

little about you. But that settles it. Tomorrow evening, I insist you come to supper. At our place." Susannah turned to her husband to see what he thought. Lucas shrugged and wiped his hands on a handkerchief.

"You can finally see the place," he offered finally. "And I'm sure my Susie wants you to know what it's like to hold a chicken."

Susannah grinned at that and turned to Jeb. Indeed, she decided, he would do perfectly. The young man needed a wife, and she was certain she could talk him into one after a good hearty meal.

Chapter Five

Brooklyn, New York; 1880

It was cold. So cold. And there was snow everywhere. Rowena glanced down at her worn out boots, scuffed and more gray than black now. They were not meant for the snow. And sometimes, she felt, nor was she.

Wrapping her cloak about her, she hurriedly crossed the street. The houses blurred into one as she went to each of them, searching for work. Lost and destitute in New York, she managed some sewing work and house work to keep from starving. But most nights, she still spent beneath the stars wondering how much longer she would last.

"I'm sorry." The woman shook her head and closed the door in her face. It was the tenth one in a row. The eleventh one had been a man who'd sent her a nasty look, so Rowena had run off before he could say anything she didn't want to hear.

Shivering, Rowena grabbed for the railing and made her way down the stairs. But the last step was covered in ice, and she slipped. Before she could catch herself, she'd fallen hard and sprawled in a stunned mess on the sidewalk.

Only when her shaking limbs forced her to start moving or give up, Rowena gathered herself up and start walking again. Having lost the courage to find more work for the day, she walked on and ended up in front of a church. She had been there a month ago, she was certain of it, and knew it was open to the poor during the day. With the last of her energy, Rowena pushed the door open.

"God bless you. How are you, my child? Come, close to the warmth," the pastor waved a hand over where he was feeding a small table set up near a fireplace in the back corner. It was a cozy place, and she felt the cold fading away.

Shrugging off a shiver, Rowena managed a small smile and nodded, obediently coming forward. With the others, also tired and dirty, she managed to eat some real food. The meat was tough and the bread was dry, but it was the best meal she'd had in weeks.

"West, see?" One of the men was handing around the newspaper. "That's where I'm going. West where all that land is, and I'm gonna own a whole lot of it. I'll build me a house and have a bunch of chickens. I'll never starve again! There's so much land out there and just anyone can take it. That's what I hear, anyway."

The old woman next to him shook her head. "You crazy old fool. That's just what you are. Crazy. Them angels are coming for us and they'll take care of us real good. You wait and see."

Rowena listened quietly and accepted the paper when

it reached her. She glanced over the advertisement the man was speaking about, and noticed there were other mentions about the west.

"Young women from East who wish to come West are welcome at our Boarding House. Rocky Ridge, Colorado. Large house with small fee. Will teach to live and make a home. Jessups of Colorado. First stop after Colorado Springs. All women welcome."

Rowena found her eyes drawn back to that one. Colorado, she hardly knew of that territory and would never find it on a map. But it was west, and it almost sounded like they were talking to her. They had a place for her to stay. She needed that in the worst way.

Biting her tongue, she tried to memorize the advert and handed over the newspaper to the one next to her. Rowena could hardly focus on anything after that, and left the building sooner than she had expected. Wrapping her blanket tightly around her, she walked and carefully counted her coins. She had to make them last, but what if she found something better than living like this?

Her courage grew, as it had since that night she had left the gambling house. The weariness faded away and she hastened to the train station. Breathless, she went up to the ticket booth and smiled at the disgruntled worker. "One ticket to Colorado, please."

"Three dollars, then."

Her smile slipped. For a minute she stared at her little coin purse. Those savings had slowly begun to disappear even though she had worked so hard to earn every penny. Swallowing hard, Rowena carefully counted out each coin. Her heart pounded and her fingers trembled, and she prayed harder than ever before that the last bit of money might last.

She couldn't help herself. If she left, she wouldn't have the money to return. There would be no choice but to go there and survive somehow. She considered changing her mind, but her tongue swelled and she couldn't talk as the man handed over her ticket.

"To your left. It leaves at half past two. Next."

Breathless, Rowena tried to compose herself. Standing back, she glanced around at everyone else preparing to take their own journey. Some of them looked excited, some looked sleepy, and some just looked cold. She shivered, and admired the thick coats. Trying to distract herself, the young woman watched the crowd grow until the train arrived.

It was so loud, and it shook the station as it drew closer. She held her bag tightly to her chest, and watched with wide eyes as it came to a halt.

"All aboard!" A man jangled a bell loudly, shouting at everyone on the platform.

Rowena jumped to attention and clutching her ticket tightly, hurried inside the car. Her eyes watched everyone pack their things away and take their seats, and she copied as she sat in the very back, keeping her head down.

The journey was long and tiring, so she hardly slept. That came from the nerves, the chill, and definitely the view outside her window. How had she not known the world was so big? It just kept going on, the land disappearing behind the horizon and over the mountains and valleys. Rowena couldn't imagine sleeping through something as exciting as this.

And before she knew it, she was there. The first stop after Colorado Springs. Rowena cautiously stepped out onto the small platform, tiny compared to the one in New York, and wondered if she had the wrong location. She walked around it in a circle, and turned to ask the conductor if she was on the wrong stop. But the whistle blew and the engine started up again, leaving her on her own.

Chapter Six

Rocky Ridge, Colorado; 1880

"Eleanor!"

"Susannah!" The two women hugged each other tightly before their husbands ushered them inside. It was a chilly evening and they turned in to where it was warm. Eleanor led them over to the cradle where little Susie was curled up in her bed.

"Oh, such a precious little one." Susannah put a hand over her heart. "Oh, isn't she an angel? Lucas, look." She turned as her husband strolled over, wrapping an arm around her waist. She smiled and turned back to the child. The little girl was nearly two years old, and growing so quickly.

Her tall brunette friend could only give her a sympathetic look. "I'm afraid we tired her out today in the garden. I'm sorry she's not awake for you."

Shrugging it off, Susannah went with them to the table. The sight of the little girl had warmed her heart, and it was such a pleasure to be watching the little girl grow up. Only a few years ago Susannah and Lucas had come to terms with the sad fact that they would never have their own children.

At least I can still have children in my life, Susannah thought gratefully. *At least I can watch them grow.* She couldn't keep the smile from her face as she looked at her husband with love and respect. They'd weathered a difficult storm and she was thankful for God's help through that time and today for her husband's unyielding love and support.

"You're looking as lovely as ever," Eleanor was saying. "Please sit. Honestly, Lucas Jessup, you have yourself quite the woman there."

Susannah didn't need to look at him to know his eyes would crinkle up. Sitting beside her, he slipped his hand over hers and squeezed it. "Indeed."

"Come sit down," Matthew pulled Eleanor closer. She complied, bringing over the bread and taking her seat. "I've been wanting to eat ever since you started on the cake."

Eleanor shot him a look. "No, I was saving that for later. For the news, remember? Goodness, you're always getting carried away."

Susannah glanced at Lucas with almost a smirk and then she looked back at Eleanor. "The news? What are you two talking about? Are you trying to hide something from us?"

Guilt spread across the woman's face for a moment before a smile finally broke through. Matthew's hand was still wrapped around hers, and they made such a pretty picture. Seeing their smiles, Susannah realized that if there was news, then it was good news.

For the hundredth time, she prayed in gratitude for having been able to bring these two wonderful people together. It reminded her of her dreams about matchmaking and building a legacy of creating families to set out on their own adventures. For now, Lucas was still thinking about her idea.

And tonight wasn't about her thoughts or ideas or plans. The smiles on her friends' faces were only growing bigger and Susannah was impatient. Whatever secret they had, it was too obnoxious now to keep quiet. Deep inside she knew what the surprise was going to be, but she wanted to hear it said aloud, anyway.

To their amazement, it was Matthew who finally gave in and spoke up. "Oh, I can't wait any longer. I don't know what you were thinking, Eleanor, about waiting until afterwards. But she—I mean we—well, there's going to be another baby." He chuckled and kissed his wife's hand tenderly. "We're going to have another child in the house. Can you believe it?"

Even though she'd known deep down what they were going to tell them, Susannah was taken aback when the actual words were out. For a moment she was spellbound, staring at them with wonder and love. She didn't even know how to respond at first. Ignoring the sudden pain in her stomach, she remembered she was glad for them. Grinning, she threw her arms up and hurried around the table. "Oh! Oh, I am so happy for you! The both of you! My, the three of you." She kissed her friend on the cheek once, twice, and three times.

She laughed as Eleanor turned red and ducked her head in for a hug. Matthew's arms wrapped around the two women as they giggled softly. Realizing her husband was missing out, Susannah pulled away and turned to Lucas.

She saw his smile, and knew it was kind. He was as happy for them as she was. But she couldn't look to his eyes. She worried that maybe there would be something there just for her that she didn't want to see. She should know by now he'd come to terms with their reality of childlessness. A tiny, unfounded fear still lingered. She longed for it to go away. Maybe one day it would.

Stepping away, she patted Eleanor's arm. "That is absolutely lovely news," Susannah sighed, and returned to her seat. "Little Susie will love being a big sister, I'm certain of it."

Eleanor bit her lip. "We're still trying to decide how to tell her. She's still so young, I'm not sure she's going to understand. But we're very excited, so thank you. I hope it's another girl. Matthew wants a boy."

"Who wouldn't?" He teased her, and passed around the ribs.

Susannah accepted the rolls from Lucas, and their hands touched for just a moment. She took a deep breath and focused now on putting food on her plate. The short celebration had tired her out, and a weariness grew in her bones as they started on supper. Though she filled her plate, her appetite disappeared and it was difficult to swallow.

As she forced food into her mouth, small bites at a time, the happy couple discussed their plans for building a larger house. Already Eleanor was planning all these games and activities for her children, and Matthew was saving up to purchase more land. It was a happy conversation for a happy future. Susannah was happy for them, but it took all her energy to not focus on her own childlessness.

Fortunately, it was cut shorter than expected since Matthew wanted Eleanor to rest early. Her husband helped her onto the wagon and they started home. Alone, they said nothing.

She thought she was tired enough to last the entire night without getting up, but shortly before dusk Susannah climbed quietly out of bed. The room felt too small, and it was so hot that she couldn't breathe. Her back protested the movement and she paused to stretch. As she did, the mattress tilted and she heard Lucas groan softly. Biting her tongue, she ducked her head and waited with a pounding heart, but he fell silent.

Wrapping herself up in a woolen cloak, Susannah staggered out to the front porch. Gasping for air, she could see her breath fog in a cloud before her as she slumped onto the bench. She wrapped her arms around herself as a dark fog of pent up emotions she'd been holding back finally escaped. Closing her eyes, Susannah could clearly see their faces again—her friends' happy faces as they announced yet another baby to be born into their little family. Soon they would have two children. Most likely, there would be more along the way as well. She knew that's what it was like, that was how families grew.

In the daylight, it was easy to recall how blessed and fortunate she was to have such a spacious home, a beautiful open land, and a good husband who cared for her. However, in the evenings, sometimes it felt like the darkness would swallow her up only to remind her of how silent their house was. No small pattering feet, no cries or innocent laughter, no children scrambling around either clean or mussed. The thought was enough to cut through her heart. For a minute she tried to take deep breaths, one after another, in and out. But on the third, she closed her eyes again and recalled how alone she was. Twenty-seven years old and after years of marriage, still childless.

She thought she had come to terms with it, knowing she would never have even one. With Lucas, the two of them had gone through a difficult time as she forced herself to accept this. Susannah tried to remind herself that she had already accepted it, but in that breath, it stuck in her throat and came out as a cry.

It was a crack that brought down her walls. The tears fled down her cheeks, and wracking sobs encased her entire body. Everything shook and she gripped herself tighter, trying to pull herself together. Sliding off the bench, she leaned against a post as her nightgown grew damp with the snow. No one was there, she told herself, and it didn't matter anymore. The façade had disappeared, and Susannah's strength had failed her.

The sun was rising before she gathered the courage to pull herself back up onto her feet. If she hadn't had strength earlier, Susannah had less now as she tried to make it to her room. Her things were damp so she changed out of her chemise and hid it before stiffly slipping back beneath the covers next to Lucas.

Still sniffling, Susannah tried to stop the shivering and prayed that her husband hadn't noticed. He would be getting up soon, and she knew he had a busy day. Closing her eyes, she tried not to touch him for fear he would notice she had been outside. Fortunately she didn't, because she would have discovered his limbs were just as cold.

Chapter Seven

Rocky Ridge, Colorado; 1880

"That was very kind of you. Thank you so much, sir, I do appreciate this. Ma'am, thank you." Rowena offered a slight curtsy as they prepared to leave her.

He tipped his hat. "Our pleasure. The Jessups are a good family. They'll take good care of you in Rocky Ridge." The kind man's wife nodded, and they started down the lane. Rowena only realized then she had forgotten their names, but by then it was too late.

They had been generous to drive her the last league of her journey. It was comforting as well, to hear good things about the Jessups. Rowena turned and crossed over the hill to find the house they'd mentioned.

"Oh." She stopped at the sight. Her heart pounded as she gaped, wondering if this was just a dream. This place was lovelier than any fairy tale she had ever dreamed of. The young woman gazed around in fascination, wondering if this was real or if she was imagining it. There was green everywhere, in the trees and the grass and reaching high into the mountains that touched the sky.

She saw a large barn nestled close where she saw pens for animals. In the middle of everything was the prettiest house that Rowena had ever seen. Beautiful oak with a stone chimney, porches wrapping all the way around with a sturdy roof and lovely flowers around the windows. Towards the back, she saw a clothesline, and a fenced area for the gardening.

Rowena finally jerked herself out of her daze and started her march to the door. Determined to succeed, she knocked on the door and was trying to gather her words when the door opened.

"Good afternoon," the short blonde woman proclaimed, and tilted her head at Rowena. All of her resolve and strength melted away, however, looking at the woman. Though she had to be older, she had the bearing of a princess and suddenly Rowena didn't know what to say. "Well, do come in," the woman offered and stepped back.

"I, um, I'm sorry," Rowena glanced at the mud she was tracking in. Stopping in the hallway, she clutched her bag. "I was, well, I was looking for the boarding house, and I don't know if I'm… I saw an ad in New York…"

The woman had been following her words and immediately brightened. Her smile grew wider as she clasped her hands excitedly. "Oh, wonderful! Well then you are most welcome. You're in the right place, dear. Please, take off your coat and put your things down."

The blonde woman took Rowena's hand and pulled

her into the warmth of the home. She couldn't believe how spacious and open the house was.

"Are you hungry? I'm making cookies. You definitely look like you could eat something right about now. Come along, come along." Rowena was seated at a large table before she knew what was going on. "I'm Susannah Jessup," the blonde woman explained. "I run this with my husband, Lucas. This is our house, and then we're working on building the boarding house all around it right now. We've had a few others stay with us, but we wanted to make it official. Oh, it's lovely having guests. You're from New York, you say?"

Shyly accepting a big cookie, Rowena nodded. "Yes. And thank you, they smell delicious."

Susannah chuckled. "Please, do eat. Goodness knows my husband and I can't eat all of these. You've certainly come a long way. Well, I suppose I can talk while you eat."

Rowena took a bite and felt her nerves calm slightly.

"Let's see. Boarding is three dollars a week, payable at the end of the week. I think that's fair and far less than what you'd pay in town at the hotel. That includes your own room and all your meals, but I do expect you to help around the house and the garden. I'm here to teach you any skills you might find necessary. My husband works in town most days, so we can take you there if you need to go. Now, do you know how long you'd like to stay?"

Swallowing, Rowena looked down. "I don't rightly know, I'm afraid. I came here because I really didn't have any other place to go. So, there's no place to go back to. I really don't know what I'm going to do next."

The enormity of her actions weighed on her shoulders again. Hesitantly she rubbed her hands together and tried to imagine what she was to do next. Get a job? Keep going further west? Where would she end up, and what would she do?

To her surprise, Susannah smiled. "Well, that's nothing to worry about. You are most welcome here for as long as you need, Miss—oh dear, I am talking too much. I'm terribly sorry, I've forgotten my manners. Whatever shall I call you?"

"Rowena," she offered, "Rowena Oakton."

Mrs. Jessup beamed at her. "Then welcome, Miss Rowena Oakton. We are most glad to have you here. Now, would you like another cookie or would you like a tour first?" And she produced such a light-hearted grin with bright eyes that Rowena nearly forgot that the woman was older than herself.

Overwhelmed with such friendly kindness, Rowena didn't know what to do. "I suppose a tour would be nice. And I'm really sorry I'm not sure how long I'll be here. A few weeks, I suppose? I'm still sorting some things out, I'm afraid."

"Don't you worry," Susannah assured her. "Things will sort out as they should. Do come along to see the house, and then we'll return for another cookie. So this is our kitchen, as you can see. There's plenty of room for all the necessary cooking, the churning." Taking Rowena's arm, she showed her about the place.

At the first bedroom they came to, Rowena put down her bag and Susannah explained where everything was. Though it was definitely a boarding house, Susannah explained, the cheap price and amenities was meant to

ensure everyone learned their independence. Guests
were granted access to exactly what they needed, no
more and no less. It was apparent that Susannah had
put together a fluid system that would work seamlessly
and allow for the least amount of work for all included
parties. It was just as fascinating as everything else at
the Jessup home and boarding house.

Rowena's courage grew as she went from one room
of the house to the next with Susannah. It turned out
that her temporary home was as lovely inside as it was
outside. Every room impressed her, from the abundant
bookshelves to the large sitting room. A cozy place with
more than enough room, she wondered as if it might be
actually be bigger than that gambling house in Manhat-
tan. She wrinkled her nose at the thought of that place,
and smiled as Mrs. Jessup looked at her.

Suddenly she realized how much easier it was to
think of good things in a wonderful atmosphere like
Rocky Ridge. Rowena dashed out thoughts of the past
and focused on the thrill of excitement running through
her veins at the prospect of living in Colorado—and far
away from New York—for the rest of her life.

After grabbing another cookie as they passed by the
kitchen, the women went outside and wound their way
down the path around the barn and garden. Every part
of the place was lovely. Idyllic, even. Rowena marveled
at her luck and part of her wished she would never need
to leave this, though she knew she couldn't live with
the Jessup couple forever.

"Well I'm sure you're tired now that you've finished
the last part of your journey," Susannah said as they returned inside. "You should rest, and we'll see you for

supper?" She patted Rowena's arm and guided her towards the hallway so she wouldn't get lost. "First door on your left, dear." And then she walked away humming.

Obediently Rowena went to the bedroom and settled on the bed. Looking around the room, she wondered at the space she had now. She'd never had a room to herself. It was so large, so clean, and currently all hers. She felt tears sting her eyes when the gravity of the events of the last few months sunk in completely. She shook the tears away and decided to just be happy to have made it to Rocky Ridge, Colorado.

Though she strongly believed she would never be able to fall asleep with all the emotions she was experiencing, the young woman's eyelids soon closed and her head nestled into the curve of a very soft pillow.

Chapter Eight

It was springtime, and three weeks had passed before Rowena knew it. Every day brought her a new adventure with lessons to learn and hard work to complete. From her days of cleaning and serving drinks at the gambling house, she adapted quickly to the necessities of housework, gardening, and sewing. She wasn't afraid of the hard work.

"You look like a queen out there," she smiled at the pink cheeks Susannah wore as she returned inside from her ride with Lucas. Rowena was making supper on her own for the first time, and with the hearty stew simmering in the cast iron pot, she had a moment's respite. Trying to look calm herself, she stepped aside to let the woman inside. "Have you been riding all your life?"

Her innocent comment made Susannah burst into laughter. "Oh goodness sakes, no. Same as you, I grew up in the city. I lived in Boston, until I was about eighteen. Or maybe it was nineteen. Gracious, I can't even really remember. Did you make cornbread?"

Rowena looked worried for a minute, and then nodded quickly. "Oh, yes. It's baking now."

Susannah grinned. "Oh, of course. I didn't notice it. Perfect, then. We're almost set, I think." She smiled and looked around the room. "You see, I answered an ad to become a wife. It's how I got here to marry Lucas. We'd been married nearly a year before he got me on a horse. I've been unsteady on them ever since, I'm afraid. Oh dear, I smell something burning."

Rowena sniffed the air with a frown. "Oh!" The young lady hurried over, realizing she had forgotten to keep stirring the stew. Grabbing a large wooden spoon, she stirred, making sure nothing was sticking to the bottom of the pot. The burning smell faded, but she frowned, having thought she'd been doing so well.

Then Susannah was there, watching carefully but silent. Rowena could feel the woman's gaze on her, and hoped she would tell her what to do, but she said nothing. "I think it will turn out all right," Rowena offered. "Most of it, I think?"

About to turn for confirmation, she glanced down to see the hot tray of cornbread growing dark brown around the edges. Reaching behind her, she picked up a towel and moved the bread onto the table. "That's better," she murmured. "Right?"

Her heart pounded, hoping she hadn't ruined everything. It had taken quite some time to prepare the meal, gathering and measuring and cutting. No one had food to waste, so she would feel truly terrible if the meal had to be thrown out because she ruined it. With a furrowed brow, she concentrated her efforts on saving the meal, and once everything was no longer burning, she turned to the table which she had yet to finish setting.

Mrs. Jessup was humming, standing over by the window. Every time she glanced towards the woman while setting up the supper table, she was still there. Just two days ago they'd had another snowfall, a light one but snow just the same. Wrapped in a shawl, Susannah was ready the moment her husband came in.

She was pouring mugs of water as Mr. Jessup came home, stamping his boots dry just outside the front door and shaking off the moisture from his hair. Rowena paused as Susannah stepped forward to help him shed his coat, and rubbed her shawl over his head to dry it. Her actions were unnecessary, but they shared smiles as they worked to dry him off.

Rowena paused and watched, wondering if they could read each other's minds, the way they said nothing. This was different than anything Rowena had seen before. Her aunt and uncle had never been this caring or well, pleasant, to each other. And it certainly was nothing like the behavior she'd seen at the gambling house, the smarmy pinches and wicked winks.

Trying to understand, she watched even though it felt as if she were intruding. Biting her lip, she tried to guess what they were saying in the silence, but she didn't know the language. Suddenly, she realized she wanted a special form of expression with a kind and loving man one day. The thought was a jolt and it made her look away quickly. Reminding herself that she didn't normally get what she wanted, she tried to push the new longing deep inside.

"Good evening, Rowena. It's good to see you. Something smells mighty good." Lucas smiled as he spoke to her and gave her a nod. She managed one back, and he busied himself by putting away his things and Susannah helped out in the kitchen. Within a few minutes, they were all seated down and enjoying supper.

That night, Rowena couldn't sleep as she thought about the way Susannah and Lucas had looked at each other. Had they done it before, and she simply hadn't noticed? Tossing and turning, she tried to make sense of it but couldn't. After a short lifetime of never seeing any married couple truly happy, she wondered if the idea of love might actually be real.

The next morning, she was still tired and distracted, and it wasn't until much later that she recalled she was supposed to be paying for rent again. Rowena glanced at Susannah who was knitting a baby blanket for a friend, and wondered why it hadn't been mentioned. Or most likely, she realized, it had been mentioned and she hadn't been paying attention.

"Pardon me," she excused herself and hurried to her room. Pulling out her bag from beneath the bed, Rowena knelt and dug through the wrinkled old thing and reached into the furthermost pocket where she'd been keeping the last of her coins. But as she felt around, she realized there weren't any there.

Inhaling sharply, Rowena frowned and tossed the bag upside down, shaking it madly. Surely there were still a few more coins. It seemed impossible, and she could hardly believe things were this bad. After all, what would she do? She'd be tossed out, and to do what? To beg on the streets? She'd been enjoying her time here so much that she hadn't given much thought again to the idea of leaving. Or of how she'd keep paying her room and board bill.

After feeling around every crevice of the bag and dumping her the contents of her reticule out on the bed, eventually Rowena managed to find a few last lingering coins and one bill. Just enough. Displaying the money in her hand, her heart felt as empty as the bag was now. Knowing she needed to tell Susannah she had to leave tomorrow left a lump in her throat. She'd have to go since she couldn't pay to stay.

But it couldn't wait, she knew. She had seen folks at the gambling house live in denial and were often physically kicked out. Rowena wouldn't be like that. Taking a deep breath, she closed a fist over the last of her money and made her way downstairs.

"Excuse me, Mrs. Jessup?" She stood in the hallway, suddenly nervous. Her heart pounded as her mouth turned dry. Rowena tried to find the right words as her boarding lady looked up with that cheerful smile. "I'm afraid I must be leaving tomorrow," she forced the words out before she could get tongue tied. "Here is the last of my rent." And she marched forward with her hand outstretched.

Susannah's surprise showed clearly. "Oh." Slowly she accepted the wadded-up bill and the coins. Rowena watched the woman look up at her. "I didn't expect you to be leaving so soon. It's only been a few weeks, surely. What are your plans? Where are you going?"

Her cheeks flamed at the questions, and she couldn't meet the woman's gaze. Not Mrs. Jessup, who had been so kind as to take her in and teach her these skills. Why, she even had another dress now besides the one she had arrived in. "Further west, I suppose. I'll just keep moving. But I, well, I don't have the money to stay with you. I can burden you no longer."

It had sounded eloquent to her, but Susannah merely squinted. "You're out of money, dear?"

She almost wished she was back at the gambling house. "I'm afraid so, ma'am." Clasping her hands together tightly, Rowena tried to hide the humiliation. "It's been lovely, but I won't be in your way any longer." There was a moment of silence as Susannah stood and looked up at her, but Rowena couldn't take it any longer. "Good night," she stammered, and left.

She went to her room and looked around. It was tidy, but it had become her home so quickly. This was the nicest place she had ever been in, and she loved every inch inside and every breath of fresh air outside. Rowena stood by her window. Where would she go now? What would she do?

Most likely back on the streets, she realized, and climbed into her bed. How was she going to handle that? With a load of questions and worries on her mind, Rowena tried to sleep but tossed and turned the night away.

Chapter Nine

The following morning, after a restless sleep, Rowena pulled herself out of bed and dressed. Slowly and carefully she packed her things into her bag, and tidied the room. Everything was set back the way it had been on the day she'd arrived, and only once she was satisfied did she leave the room. She closed the door slowly, and took a deep breath.

After gathering her resolve, she headed down the stairs. It was time she was on her way. Rowena glanced around as she reached the ground floor and found Susannah bustling about the kitchen, her hair pulled back and her apron around her waist. She was marching back and forth, taking the cooking utensils over to the sink. Only on her third round did she notice Rowena at the stairs.

"Well! It's about time you were waking up," she brightened and shifted everything in her arms to wave Rowena forward. "Come in, get yourself some breakfast. I made us hot cakes."

Reluctantly she stepped forward, grabbing her bag

with both hands. Wavering on the line of whether or not she should be eating there, Rowena glanced towards the front door. She couldn't intrude here if she were no longer a paying customer, after all. No matter what was said, that relationship of buyer and seller came first. Integrity was still important. She took a deep breath and prepared to talk, but Mrs. Jessup beat her to it.

"You packed already? Nonsense. Now put that down, Rowena. Come sit down and let's enjoy us something delicious to break our fast. Besides, I have something to speak to you about."

For some reason, that set the hair on her neck on end. But she didn't know what else to do so she gently set her bag down and rubbing her tingling arm, Rowena took a seat. Susannah sat across from her, still smiling as though it were nothing serious.

Neither of them talked as they carefully dished out hot cakes and bacon onto their plates, Rowena slow and particular and Susannah quick and efficient as ever. Mrs. Jessup offered grace, and then had a few bites before noticing her young boarder was only staring at her food, unable to touch it. Taking a quick sip of her tea, Susannah set her utensils down.

"You don't need to leave, you know," she told her kindly. "You're more than welcome to stay here. Why, with your help in the garden, we could easily expand it and start selling more at the market. It's not as if we're struggling, of course, but that's none of your concern. But as long as you don't have a plan, you might as well stay with us. That's what we're here for, after all."

Shaking her head, Rowena stared at the food. "I

won't take your charity, but thank you. I should be going soon."

"But I mean it," Mrs. Jessup shook her head. "My advert said it. I want to help young women find a better future." Waving her hands in the air, she attempted to explain. "That's why I opened the boarding house, it's for young women who are coming through, passing by. You know, to come west and meet their men and settle into their new lives."

She was patting Rowena's hand when her words sunk in. What was that second part? She furrowed her brow and looked at Susannah who was talking about hope and cheer. "What did you mean, meeting men?"

Mrs. Jessup looked at her through wide eyes and with an open mouth. "Well, you know, of course. I mean, I thought I put it plainly. Well, without saying everything, granted, but the point was made that… About mail order brides. It's not easy, after all, arriving out here from the city to find yourself in a new strange place without friends, and not even knowing what you're supposed to be able to do."

As she spoke, trying to explain herself, the truth came out, though a bit jumbled and somewhat evasive. It made more sense, explaining some of their conversation they'd had in the past. Susannah had attempted to address a few things, like the handsome men at church, and someday having children. But Rowena had brushed everything off, since Susannah married and had made the mention of having no children. Now, her pulse quickened as she considered what the woman was telling her.

This was a boarding house for single women. A place

for them to stay while they waited to find a man and get married. Not just to offer room and board, but to be sent off into marriage.

Inhaling sharply, Rowena stood up quickly, away from the table. "You never said such a thing!" She interrupted the woman in dismay, shaking her head. "How could you be so dishonest?"

Such words paled Susannah Jessup. Rowena was crestfallen, wondering why everyone needed to be so devious and secretive about their true motives. Wrapping her arms around herself, she wondered if that was just the way the world operated.

"I'm sorry," Susannah called for her as the younger woman was grabbing her bag. "Please, stop. Rowena, I apologize. I didn't mean to… I just assumed you understood what I was trying to do. Well, I supposed you just wanted to be quiet about making a match, or perhaps you had decided to think of finding a mate when you felt more stable. I wasn't sure, but I didn't want to intrude. So I waited."

Rowena looked at her with continued distrust. She was still angry and not interested in giving it up just yet.

"Please, allow me to fix this. Will you?" Susannah took a step towards her and smiled weakly.

With a groan, Rowena stared at her boots. Shoulders slouched, she clutched her bag and shrugged. A hopelessness settled over her shoulders, and she didn't know what to do. "Fix what?"

Taking a deep breath, Mrs. Jessup came over and set the carpet bag back down on a chair. She did so carefully, patting it before turning to study Rowena thoughtfully. "My advert wasn't as honest as I thought it would be, and I should have done better. I can admit to that. So I understand the confusion."

Rowena raised an eyebrow and nodded.

"My boarding house is, as I said, to help women get on their feet as they transition homes and livelihoods. Whether you have come for a husband or not, you are most welcome here. We would love your company, and we could always use your help until you decide where to go next."

After a deep breath, Rowena tried to set aside the rising anger. Besides, it was hard to ignore the hopeful smile that Susannah Jessup was giving her. It was better than having nowhere else to go, she reminded herself. And this was a very generous apology. She'd received few apologies in her life and it felt nice to be cared for enough to receive one. Less than a minute later, she melted and nodded shyly. "I suppose that's all right."

"Oh good!" Susannah chuckled and clapped her hands together. "Then I don't need to eat all of this by myself. Now sit yourself back down, and eat up. We have a busy day ahead of ourselves."

Obediently Rowena did just that, but not as happily as Susannah would have hoped. Her grip on her mug was so tight that she had to hold it with both hands. The more she thought about it, the more infuriated she was by such deception. How could Susannah have treated her so kindly with all these lies? Life really wasn't that different outside the gambling house, she realized, with people lying and still conning each other.

After eating, she put her bag back in her room and returned to clean up the table. Her musings kept her mind occupied as she tried to figure out what her next move should be. From the sound of it, she could stay until she was married. Marriage! The idea was horrendous and laughable all in one, for tying herself to a man was a terrifying thought. Trusting a man with her safety and happiness was madness. Men could be abusive, loud, and greedy. Why would she want such a thing?

She shook her head, unable to believe it even after considering it for a few hours. There was nothing she could do just then, she admitted, so she would stay for a short while. Rowena stared at the plants around her in the lovely garden. She had no money and no place to go. Rowena leaned down and grabbed a particularly nasty weed, pulling it free.

The idea of leaving stayed with Rowena, and she knew she had to start on a plan, and soon. Susannah and Rowena worked quietly, both lost in their thoughts. Yet they both considered the same thing, of whether men should have a place of importance in Rowena's life.

Chapter Ten

Susannah forced herself to consider the flaws in her plan, and ran through the steps in case she had missed something. Walking around the kitchen stirring the batter gave her the time she needed to think about it, but it appeared the same. It had become apparent that Rowena had not come here to meet a particular man, as they had discussed. But this didn't mean that she didn't want to be married, she reasoned to herself. The girl was still so young and surely had a desire to find a man to settle down with.

On top of that, the young woman needed someone to care for her. She needed the security marriage offered. And whether she knew it or not, Susannah knew Rowena needed the sheer joy of being in love.

Besides, the invitation had already been given and there wasn't time to retract it. Nor would she do such a thing, turn down a dear friend like that. Susannah wrinkled her nose and glanced towards the windows, watching the sun beginning to set. They should be arriving any moment, and dessert still wasn't prepared.

Shaking her head slightly, Susannah set the cake batter into the pan, and took it to her stove. Once it was safely inside, she hastened over to Rowena who was carefully mashing the chopped potatoes.

"How do they look? Just about ready?" She glanced over Rowena's shoulder to see her progress.

Rowena took a deep breath and offered a lopsided grin. She was a lovely young lady with dark hair, darker eyes, and the cutest little chin. "Lumpy but delicious?"

Susannah gave her a look, reminding her that they were working on her answering questions with real answers, not another question. It made Rowena chuckle and shrugging, she added a little more pepper. "There. I think that will do. We won't go hungry, and that's the important thing." Something flashed in the woman's eye before she left to put them in the pot over the fire.

"I suppose," Susannah mused to herself, not knowing how else to answer such a comment. They finished up supper then, stirring the carrots and parsnips, and setting the table.

That's when she heard a knock and hurried over to find Matthew and Eleanor there. Susannah beamed, letting her friends in. Rowena stood back like a shadow before being introduced, and everyone stepped into the kitchen. They were hardly in before Susannah heard a creak and a thump of boots. Her heart pattered and she turned around.

"Something smells delightful," Lucas called, announcing his presence with Jeb Harbin beside him.

Susannah waved. "Come in, then. Supper is ready and waiting."

Jeb followed behind her husband. After carefully setting his hat down as well, she watched him put a hand on his vest as though he were wondering about taking that off, too. Holding back a chuckle, she patted Jeb on his arm. "There's no need to stress, dear. It's just supper with friends. It's really just another supper at the Jessup home and you've done that more than once. And those always go well, don't they?"

He smiled. "Yes, ma'am, they certainly do."

"Rowena," she caught the girl's attention. "I'd like you to meet Rocky Ridge's deputy, Mr. Jeb Harbin. He's been in town for nearly three years, and is building a home right now. Mr. Harbin, this is Miss Rowena Oakton from New York City, she's a guest in our house and is fastidiously becoming a better gardener than me."

As hoped, the young girl blushed and she shook her head. "You're much too kind."

"And Jeb, you already know Matthew and Eleanor. Let's be seated, shall we?" Everyone went to the loaded table right away. Lucas pulled out her seat, and she beamed at the party. "Jeb, how would you like to say Grace?"

"I'd be honored, Miss Susannah." He bowed his head and waited a moment for the others to do the same. "Dear Lord, we thank You for the bounty on this table. All things come from You and for Your love and care, we're truly grateful. I thank You for the friends, old and new, around this table. May we never forget that You have a plan. Amen."

Susannah smiled at Jeb's prayer. Apparently, he was thankful to have met Rowena. As the mashed potatoes made it to her, she heaped a spoonful on her plate. She hoped Jeb enjoyed them. She studied their guests carefully, watching and waiting. All she wanted was a sign, something that told her they were interested in one another. Rowena was hard to read, but she hoped she was right that Jeb's prayer meant what she thought it did.

"Matthew, how are the horses?" Lucas brought up conversation to fill in the silence.

The man nodded. "Doing just dandy. It's a lot of work which isn't a bad thing, but since we're also trying to prepare for the arrival of our next babe, well, it's easy to get distracted." He chuckled and winked at his wife.

"I keep telling him that I can still do the work," she turned to Rowena. "But men don't tend to listen very well."

There was light laughter as Matthew objected. Then Jeb spoke, offering a hesitant smile. "If you really need some help, I'd be glad to offer an extra set of hands. Might be nice to have a change of pace, and all." He trailed off, and Susannah saw his gaze turn back to Rowena. Again. Her heart pounded hopefully.

Jeb's gaze turned to Rowena's often, and she seemed to be blushing more often than not. Susannah could hardly keep the smile off her face.

"So you're from New York, then?" Eleanor asked the young lady kindly, making sure she had a chance to talk to Rowena that evening. "I haven't been there often, but I remember there was much to do there."

Taking a deep breath, Rowena offered what Susannah thought was a rather tight smile. "It was busy," the young woman explained, "but I must say, I'm quite glad to be away from it. There's nothing like an open sky and not needing to elbow your way through a crowd." She smiled sincerely, finally.

Susannah finally relaxed and grinned. "There's something special about the west. Do you think you'll be staying out here, then?" Her eyes drifted over to Jeb who listened carefully, his gaze focused on Rowena.

She didn't notice the strange look Rowena gave her. "I suppose it's much too soon to say for sure. Have you been here long, Eleanor?" The topic was diverted then, off of Rowena for most of the evening.

Conversation came and went. Once most of the food was gone and no one was reaching for anything more, Susannah stood to clean up, but Lucas wrapped a hand around her waist. "Leave it," he suggested. "Why don't we take a walk? Matthew, you can see the posts I've been working on." He went to get their jackets.

"What a wonderful idea," Eleanor exclaimed. It was a good one, Susannah had to admit, and she wondered how she hadn't thought of it. Brushing it from her mind, she beamed as Jeb returned with a shawl for Rowena. Lucas must have helped him with that.

She shared a look with him then, trying to confirm with him that this was indeed a good choice to be making, that matchmaking was something she could do. But Lucas's expression was an impassive one and she had to let it go as the two of them led the way outside.

It was a good night, she reminded herself, one filled with friends and happiness. Glancing back, she watched Rowena close the gate, and Jeb was lingering nearby. For a moment it made Susannah want to turn back and help them come together.

But that's not how it worked, and she knew that. Like it had been for Eleanor and Matthew, she needed to step back and give them some time to consider one

another. Jeb was her first client, and she wanted to do
well and right by him. Rowena had become the wild-
card, however, since she hadn't sounded thrilled about
finding a husband.

A strange notion, Susannah decided, though one she
had to understand for herself. She hadn't expected to
get married, and especially to a stranger. But because
of her enormous luck and God's help, of course, she
had found the perfect match in Lucas. She wanted to
provide as much as she could for other young women.
Even if they didn't think they wanted it.

Her thoughts wandered as Lucas left her to talk with
Matthew about the posts off the path. As they went, El-
eanor reached Susannah and the two girls linked arms.
"Your Mr. Jessup has it much too good, with this lovely
house and a pretty woman to come home to every day."
She grinned teasingly and Susannah rolled her eyes.

"Enough about me. Your baby is due quite soon. How
are you doing, really?"

"Good," Eleanor told her emphatically. "I assure you,
I am. It's nearly unreal, after little Susie and being sick
constantly. But I have energy, and I can still eat everything. There are occasions where I feel queasy, but for
the most part, I'm happy. Besides, I didn't come here
tonight to discuss me. What do you think of Jeb and
Rowena?"

Susannah couldn't help but glance back at Rowena
and Jeb who were walking slower than the rest of their
party. They stood a good distance apart, and it was hard
to tell whether or not they were even talking. But she
did notice Jeb kept looking over at her.

She smiled, biting her lip. "I've already looked

through a few other options for Jeb. And once I knew for sure Rowena didn't have anyone waiting on her, well… I wanted to try. They look very nice together, don't you think?

"There's always a chance," Eleanor nodded.

"I hope so," Susannah sighed.

Chapter Eleven

It was obvious what was going on the moment Mr. Jeb Harbin arrived. Rowena's heart had beat anxiously since she had set eyes on him, knowing why he was there. Though the Jessups had mentioned they were having guests over for supper, which had happened a few times since she had arrived there, she had expected nothing more than a gathering of friends.

To invite an unmarried young man was much too obvious, especially since Susannah had confessed the true purpose of her boarding house. She shook her head in near disbelief. She was, however, becoming quite aware of the bold streak in Mrs. Susannah Jessup.

Where did such ideas stem from? Rowena didn't understand and had difficulty paying attention during supper because of this. But not wanting to be a rude guest, she had participated in conversation, and even spoken to Jeb a few times.

The man was handsome, that couldn't be denied by any woman who had eyes. As a young woman, she couldn't ignore that. His brown hair shone in the light and though it sat longer than most men's trims, it defined his strong jawline and his sharp cheekbones. He was clean shaven tonight with soft eyes. She couldn't see their color since they were too far away. Overall, the man appeared kind.

By the time they finished eating, she supposed everything was well and done so they would be leaving. Her heart dropped at the mention of a walk, and somehow Rowena found herself outside with Mr. Jeb Harbin. Lucas and Matthew had wandered off, and the other two women had linked arms like the close friends they were to whisper.

Rowena had been thinking to herself how nice it might have been to have had someone like that growing up, a close friend who knew her and her heart inside out. Looking back, there had been few friends. There had been an orange cat that belonged to her neighbors when she lived with her aunt and uncle. When she had first arrived at the gambling house, the other women had been gentle and kind to her, but that had vanished when she joined them out on the gambling house floors.

"It's a nice night," a soft voice interrupted her thoughts.

Forcing herself not to jump, she tugged on her shawl and glanced over to find Jeb not too far away. Something inside her slumped. Of course, this wasn't over yet. Swallowing the lump in her throat, Rowena tried to think kinder thoughts. He wasn't mean after all, not yet. "Indeed," she agreed finally, throwing away her fear. "The stars are bright."

His smile widened as though he achieved something just by hearing her talk. "Almost as bright as your eyes."

The statement was bold, and he hurriedly dropped his gaze as she looked at him in surprise. "I, um, hope that wasn't too forward. I apologize if…" He trailed off, stumbling over his words.

"It's fine," she interrupted, using a gentler voice than she expected. "That's kind of you."

Their steps fell together and they walked slowly beside one another. Jeb had stepped a little closer, but he gave her enough space that they didn't touch. Rowena's heartbeat slowed, and her dread faded into curiosity. After they had reached and passed the barn, she found herself stealing glances in his direction, wondering what he was thinking.

The man had talked enough during supper about the house he was building and how he wanted to build his farm. It was an interesting concept, she had considered, and had listened to his decisions. From what the other couples mentioned, Jeb had a sound idea for his future.

She could hear his breathing, she realized. Rowena glanced at him, wondering what he was looking at. His gaze had been turned down, but he started to turn towards her, and hurriedly she jerked her head away, to look at the sky. Biting her lip, she hoped he hadn't noticed.

He didn't say anything. Ahead of them, Eleanor and Susannah burst out into giggles, leaning onto one another. It was as though being together gave those two women more energy, and she shook her head. With all the extra work they had done, Rowena was more than exhausted. When another yawn came her way, she could no longer hide them.

"Oh, you're tired," Jeb stated the obvious, and stopped. She found herself doing the same as he put out a hand to her. "There's no need to tire yourself out. Hold on a moment." He gave her a nod before hastening off. Confused, she watched him catch up to Susannah, tell her something, and then he came back to her.

Rowena was just scolding herself for obeying him without even thinking about it. Jeb reached her, and put out an arm. "May I escort you, that is, back to the house? There's no need to exhaust yourself this evening." His other hand motioned back the way they had come.

She wanted to say yes, but her voice got stuck in her throat at the sight of his extended arm. Immediately unease filled her gut, and she instinctively took a step away from him. What was it with men wanting to have women with them all the time?

With a tight smile, she clutched her shawl tighter and nodded. But Rowena didn't take his arm. Taking a deep breath and looking at the path they had taken, she started forward. She didn't watch Jeb as he scrambled to catch himself and followed after her. After he stumbled twice, Rowena grudgingly slowed down so he could catch up.

Then she made space for him to walk on the path beside her. Not close enough to touch, of course, but close enough. Eventually she chanced a shy glance at him, hoping he wasn't mad at her. The man had seemed nice enough, and she didn't want to upset him. She just didn't want to be that close to him, or any man.

His brow was furrowed as he stared at the ground,

a studious expression on his face as though he were studying the ground. The man appeared so serious, that suddenly everything seemed silly. So silly that a small giggle escaped her lips.

As he turned to her, she looked away. Tightening her grasp on the shawl, she made a face at herself. What was going on with her? Shaking her head, Rowena cleared her thoughts. He was a nice man, possibly the sort of gentleman that she had heard about. Smart and quiet, he knew when not to talk and was still kind. He was even a good walking partner, she decided as they reached the big house again.

It would be inappropriate if he came inside with her since they didn't have anyone else with them, so Rowena knew he wouldn't follow after once she went through the door. But she wanted to say something to express her gratitude. As she turned to thank him, she stumbled on the steps. Her heart skipped a beat and she gasped. When she reached out to catch herself, he was already there.

"Careful," he mumbled, holding her shoulders firmly and helping her stand straight. The moment she was steady, he let go and stepped away. It was as if he understood her.

Mouth still hanging open, Rowena blinked. "I—well, thank you. For catching me and for walking me back to the house," she added carefully. "That was kind of you. I apologize for taking you away from your friends."

Shuffling his feet, he gave her a grin. It was a devilish one, such a smile that she didn't want to trust, but the crinkle in his eyes told her she could. "I didn't mind at all. I think they all had enough to talk about without me."

Her eyes followed the movement of his arm as he rubbed the back of his neck self-consciously. "Surely you would have had something to say about the posts, for the fences?" She volunteered. Though she didn't know why she was starting conversation, but standing here on the porch with him, suddenly she wasn't sure she wanted to go inside. "I'm assuming, that is, you'll need to be prepared to set them up as you start your farm."

Taking a deep breath, he shrugged. "I'd like to think that, yes, but I don't think I'm there yet. I don't have animals that need fencing. And whatever I do, it'll be much smaller than this, I'm afraid." He motioned to the house around them.

Her eyes followed the motion. "It's very nice," she admitted. "But small can still be good. And I'm sure you'll sort out the acres and the animals soon enough."

"Soon enough," he echoed, and gave her a curious look. For once, she met his gaze and wondered what Mr. Jeb Harbin was thinking as he looked at her. Usually it was easy to tell, and it made her want to crawl right out of her skin. But this time it was different, as though he weren't seeing her like something at the market. "Well, I don't want to hold you up any longer. I'll bid you good night."

He said the last part without stammering, and it made her smile. Nodding, she gave him the same invitation. "Good night, Mr. Harbin." She turned away and had one hand on the door before he cleared his throat.

"Would you join me for church?" Jeb spoke up hurriedly, taking a step forward. There was still a distance between them as Rowena turned. That's when she noticed his eyes were a soft hazel, with flecks of green in them. For a moment they were all she could see.

"Sure." The reply slipped out before she knew what she was doing. A small frown settled on her lips as she stepped back, wondering what she had just signed up for. But Jeb was already grinning that appealing smile.

Nodding, he took a deep breath as he played with the end of his jacket. "Good. I mean, great. That's just— that's good. I can… Um, I'll be here bright and early then. On Sunday morning, I mean. All right. Well, good night," Jeb offered sheepishly.

Rowena offered a tight smile as she hurried inside, saving both of them from more embarrassment. Her cheeks aflame, she made it to her room as it sunk in. She had just agreed to spend time with him again. Her heart hammered. What if Susannah and Lucas weren't around? What if it was just the two of them?

Frowning, the young woman wondered exactly how church worked. She had been inside a few chapels, and she'd certainly found meals at churches in New York, but she'd never attended a sermon. There had been preachers on soapboxes, but they had yelled and were red in the face, having nothing good to say about anyone. The Jessups went every week and always invited her, but she offered to tend to the animals instead.

Except this Sunday she would be going to church with a stranger. She tried to take a deep breath and wondered what she had gotten herself into. He had caught

her off guard, and now she had to live with the conse-
quences. Biting her lip, Rowena just hoped it went better than her imaginations were suggesting.

Chapter Twelve

"It's fine, it's fine, I'm fine, we're fine," Susannah murmured to herself with every brushstroke through her hair. Then she took a deep breath, closing her eyes. But even as she squeezed them tight, a tear escaped and hurriedly she scrubbed it away.

This was a slow morning, as it had been for the last couple of weeks. As the Jessups had come upon their wedding anniversary, Susannah was surprised to find things getting harder with time and not easier. This turn of events was most unexpected. Glancing at the downturned mirror on her nightstand, she pursed her lips and stared at her hairbrush.

It looked full, and she couldn't recall if she had cleaned it out recently or if this was accumulated from earlier brushes. But she wouldn't be surprised, she mused with a sigh, that she was losing her hair. Clearly she hadn't lost enough, and it would be the next thing to go. Her long blonde hair, her pride and joy since she had nothing else. When it was loose, it flowed down her back and over her shoulders like a cascading waterfall. Lucas loved her hair and feeling his fingers running through her tresses was a pleasure she couldn't imagine not having. It was a blessing to have this gift.

But oh, how she would trade this blessing for another. Her arms grew tired and she dropped the brush on the bed, not even bothering to put it away. Usually she had at least another hundred strokes to go, but today Susannah simply didn't have the enthusiasm.

It was their seventh anniversary. Lucas was already up to feed the animals, but she couldn't gather the vigor to do anything. She should, she knew, make something hearty and delicious for breakfast. But the idea only made her sigh at the effort. Besides, what if Lucas decided to go to town? She wouldn't blame him since she had hardly been good company lately.

The man was used to the quiet, Susannah figured, after the stories he shared about spending months on end out in the desert or the woods. He didn't really need anyone. A man married to build a family, so in that standard she had become useless to him and it was as though nothing had changed.

Another tear as her spirits plummeted.

Scrubbing her face dry, Susannah took a deep breath as she heard something move. Standing up, she frowned and glanced towards the door. Was it Lucas, finished with the chores? For a moment she waited and wondered if he would come to her. With another sigh, she realized he was probably looking for something to eat for the day.

She knew she was a pitiful sight, and tried to take a deep breath. Rubbing her cheeks, Susannah tried to find the strength, but realized she had spent everything she had. Even now, every part of her body was crying out to curl up in bed, buried beneath those blankets. It was still cold outside, with a bit of snow still on the ground in places. The cold seemed to seep into the house through the cracks.

Grudgingly she snatched up her shawl and after tugging out a wrinkle in her dress, Susannah slowly made her way to the kitchen. Hoping he wouldn't notice the extra redness in her face, she tried to think of something simple she could make them for breakfast. Eggs would be easy enough, and perhaps some bacon would be sufficient.

Caught up in her thoughts, Susannah didn't notice the smells or the sight in the kitchen until she was halfway in and bumping into a chair. Clutching it, she blinked and found Lucas watching her from beside the stove. The man was wearing one of his inscrutable gazes, and she stared numbly as he finally turned to the stove. The door squeaked open, and Susannah couldn't stop staring as she watched her husband carefully flipping bacon and eggs in the cast iron pan.

"Happy wedding anniversary," he said at last, breaking the silence.

Her voice failed her as she noticed the table, already set with their nicest plates. They were so nice that she often hated to use them. But here they were now, surrounded by fresh muffins, the eggs, and a bowl of berries. To the side, she even noticed the box of chocolates, something he always brought her for special occasions. In the middle of it all sat a lovely bouquet of greenery, so soft she couldn't help but reach out and touch one of the branches.

"It's so nice," she whispered at last. Shaking her head, she sighed. She knew she didn't deserve any of this.

Lucas stood there, eyes watching as he waited for her to say something else. Anything else. But she didn't know what. "It should be a day we celebrate," he said at last. "I wanted to ensure that we treated it properly." He meant it positively, but saw the light begin to fade from her eyes.

She knew that, but hadn't managed to do a thing. It was different than last year, she recalled, along with nearly every year before that. Such an occasion should be celebrated, and she was failing terribly. "You did a lovely job," she murmured.

He chose words carefully so that they weren't wasted nor misinterpreted. Lucas stood for a moment trying to gather his thoughts. Finally, Susannah watched him move around the table, and pulled out the chair for her. "Please, sit," he offered.

The man's hand touched her arm, guiding without pushing as Susannah took her seat. Both hands tightly clutching the shawl, the woman shook her head. "It's too nice," Susannah told him, and scrambled to wipe another tear away before he noticed.

Yet it was clear in his actions that he did. Lucas knelt beside her on his knees, pulling her hands down as he carefully held her face to rub away the sprinkling of tears with his thumbs. Ashamed, Susannah met his gaze with caution and was as surprised as she was relieved to see the softness in his eyes. His tender touch should have been telling enough.

"You are beautiful," he told her, his voice raw. Lucas

cleared his throat and continued, his hands still on her to ensure that she met his gaze. "You are my wife. And you are enough. More than."

She continued to look into his eyes, comforted.

"Today is our wedding anniversary, and it's going to be a beautiful day, no matter what we do and no matter what happens. We don't need anything or anyone else to be happy, Susannah darling, as long as we have each other." At last he curled his lips up into a smile. "And now we're going to enjoy breakfast, and hope that I haven't failed you in this manner."

Sniffling, she snorted on accident and they dissolved into tentative laughter together. Her snort and his admission of worry over his questionable cooking skills helped remove some of the tension she felt.

Though he had helped her on occasion in the kitchen, Susannah couldn't recall any occasion where he had made a meal for them before. As she swallowed the lump in her throat and nodded he moved to take his seat. It made her face feel cold now, without his warmth there, but she knew he was close enough.

He offered the blessing, and they ate quietly. The eggs were a little too salty and the muffins slightly burned, but everything tasted delightful to Susannah. For the first time in days she enjoyed eating, and slowly her misery wafted away as she began to straighten her shoulders and hold her head up high when she felt Lucas's gaze on her.

"Thank you," she said finally, meeting his eyes. "I'm sorry about the last few days. I've been...distracted." Susannah didn't know what to say, knowing that the truth of her thoughts would only make them both miserable. And he didn't deserve that. "But this was delicious, and I'm sorry I didn't do it myself. I should have tried, but I don't have anything for you this year."

Raising a hand to prevent her rambling, Lucas shook his head and gave her a small smile. "Susie darling, it's enough that you're here. And I know it's been hard," he added carefully. "There are some things, I believe, that will never get easier for us."

In that gaze he gave her, it told her everything. It told her that he knew exactly what was going on, that he had seen her tears as much as she had tried to hide them, and that he knew exactly what she was going through. Susannah's breath caught in her throat as he carefully handed over the chocolates, which had a small envelope resting on top.

Confused, she accepted both and stared at the small letter. It was clearly his handwriting, and it said her name across the front. But why was he writing her something, when he could simply say it? Lucas stood up as she frowned and set the chocolates aside to review the letter.

To her surprise, it wasn't words. Instead, they were pictures. A blueprint, to be exact. From the looks of it, it was their house. She frowned, trying to understand what sort of message this was supposed to be.

After a minute, she started to see. There were black lines for where the house already stood. But there were blue lines now, as well, showing what was to be added onto the building, to make it larger. With a furrowed brow, she looked over the four pages but only the postscript on the fifth was what told her what she hadn't understood at first. "The Jessup Boarding House for Women?"

Her arms felt heavy and she dropped everything in her lap to look at her husband. During that time, he was returning to her side, taking the seat beside her. Lucas looked at her with that intense gaze of his, making the scar on his cheek look more red than usual. Right now his eyes were a bold green, Susannah noticed, and wondered if he meant this. It was a grand gesture, she knew, but an idea that he had been resistant about.

"Do you mean it?" She asked softly. "Do you really?"

"I do." He took her hands in his. "I really do."

The pain faded away as she found her heart filled with the love that she brushed aside. So focused on what she didn't have, Susannah had ignored what she already had. With a shaky breath, she put the papers down and pulled him into a big hug, wrapping herself around him.

"You are too good to me," she murmured breathlessly against his shoulder. "I don't deserve you."

A chuckle rumbled through his body and she couldn't help but smile. "Nonsense," he told her. "You are more than enough for me and you're the most deserving woman I know. You deserve all that's good. And if this is what it takes to remind you how much I love you, then I'll do anything you like."

Smiling, she pulled back just enough to see his face. "That's an awfully big promise there, Lucas."

He was grinning as well, and the look made her heart melt. There were few people he grinned for, and that one was just for her. "Then it's a good thing I mean it, Susie darling."

Unable to restrain herself, she pulled him close for a kiss. "I love you," she told him firmly.

"And I love you," he responded.

Chapter Thirteen

She could hardly sleep through the night, let alone focus on her breakfast. Lucas was already gone and Susannah was taking care of her ill horse, so Rowena had the kitchen to herself. There had been bread and jam waiting for her on the table, and she ate two pieces but left crumbs everywhere. It took her a while to notice, and she hurried to clean up her mess before anyone came back.

Glancing out the kitchen window, Rowena saw that Susannah was carrying a pail of water into the barn. If she was there and Mr. Jessup was in town, then it would definitely be a day she had to herself.

Well, mostly. She frowned, thinking of her agreement with Mr. Harbin. Jeb. Today was Sunday, the Sabbath, and he was supposed to take her to church. But there had been no clear time, and she didn't know what to expect or how to prepare. There were so many questions on her mind now that she didn't know where to start on them.

"The sun is up." She glanced out the window and

spoke to herself. "So any later, and it won't be considered early anymore. Or perhaps he meant any time that was before the noonday meal?" Rowena was running her hands through her hair when she heard a knock on the front door.

It made her jump and she bumped into the table. The butter knife clattered off the plate and she hurriedly put it back before starting for the door. Glancing down, she hoped her dress would do. It was the nicer one she had, scrapped from an old dress of Susannah's with more lace that she had practiced her sewing on. The project had gone so well that the woman let her keep it. They had added a bottom ruffle so that it was long enough, and she enjoyed the soft material against her skin.

But as she opened the door, she found Jeb wearing something even nicer. Well, for the most part, since she noticed the elbow patches and the worn collar. But it was a suit with a jacket and a tie. He even had cufflinks, she noticed, if mismatched. His hair was slicked back, but already a few strands were falling into his face as he looked at her and smiled.

It was a nice smile, she had forgotten. "Good morning."

"Good morning," she responded.

He took a deep breath, but paused as he didn't know what else to say. Clutching his hat with both hands, Jeb looked at her with his silly grin. But she dropped his gaze, feeling awkward as she leaned against the doorframe. He shifted his weight and cleared his throat. "You look, um, you look beautiful. I mean, you are beautiful. If you don't mind my saying so."

Her nose twitched, because it sounded like he

couldn't decide what he wanted to say to her. Stammering through his compliments, she wondered if he had practiced them or had simply thought them up on the spur of the moment. It was hard to tell. But she thanked him all the same. "That's kind of you to say. I wasn't sure if this was appropriate for church," she added. "We won't be late, will we?"

Snapping to attention, he straightened and then nodded. And to confuse her, he also shook his head. "We won't be," Jeb answered her second question. The man took a deep breath to say something else, but nothing more came out. She gave him a curious look as he stiffly stepped out of the way to allow her through.

They walked together but not touching. The unease in her stomach subsided, though Rowena glanced towards the barn and almost wished that Susannah would call her back. In the two minutes they'd had of conversation that morning, Susannah had explained she wouldn't be able to attend church because of her horse. Rowena had shyly mentioned that Jeb had invited her and the woman offered advice before hurrying back out the door.

Be friendly, she'd said, to everyone that you meet. There should be familiar faces from your occasions in town. Stand when they sing, and bow your head for prayers. Just do what Jeb does or follow the others in the service. It would be rude not to do the same as everyone else. And that was all.

It wasn't very helpful advice, Rowena worried, since she had no idea what she was getting herself into. But with a soft sigh, she reached the wagon that Jeb had brought. It had a high step and he quietly offered her his arm. For a minute she wavered, wondering if she should just turn back. What was she thinking, accepting an offer to spend some time alone with this man? And in church, no less. Didn't she need an escort? Again she looked back to Susannah, who had paused and waved for a moment before reentering the barn.

Now, Rowena was alone. Well, mostly. Her gaze flickered onto Jeb's and she grudgingly accepted his grasp as he helped her into the wagon. Lucas had done the same for her a half dozen times, but Jeb was a little taller and more gentle than firm. Still, she found herself seated on the wagon seat as Jeb joined her on the other side, and they headed into town.

It was a long ride, a quiet one. His horse was beautiful and it was indeed a lovely day. Rowena found herself studying the landscape and looking around them as they went. Jeb said nothing for the most part, though she could feel his gaze on her often.

They were nearing town when he finally moved one hand from the reins and pointed behind a hill. "See that? Over the crest, that's where I'm building my home." He nodded to himself. "I've built the groundwork, and most of the walls are up. But the roof is the tricky part and I haven't quite learned that yet."

She decided it was strange, hearing a man share what he didn't know. "I'm sure you'll have it finished in no time," she assured him, not knowing what else to say.

Jeb nodded again. "That's what I'm hoping. It's difficult to make a house sturdy enough to last the winters here. I'd hate to start again," he added with a chuckle. "Especially with the harvest on its way. Oh, and here we are. See that little white building?"

"That's the church?" She asked, and he smiled. This time, it wasn't towards her however, but as though the very building made him happy.

After putting the horses in the small pasture, Jeb guided her into the building, side by side but not touching. Rowena's gaze was so focused on the people around them that were mingling and talking, dressed in nicer gowns than she had ever owned, it took her a moment to realize something had changed as they stepped inside.

Everything quieted to a low murmur, she marveled as Jeb guided her to open seats. The two of them watched as the room filled up with people, and the windows were opened for fresh air. It was different than the few chapels she had been inside in New York, less gray and with happier people. Her heart felt full, and Rowena hardly even noticed the stares.

"Good morning. And welcome one and all." The pastor walked to the pulpit with a large book. He limped but the man was wearing a wide smile as he looked around at the many faces before him. To her surprise, he even smiled at her. Rowena shifted anxiously, and worried what that meant. "It is good to see all of you here today," the man continued, "whether you are old or new friends. All are welcome in the house of God. Let us begin with Hymn 37, shall we?"

In a flutter of movements, everyone obeyed and began to pull out books from their pockets and bags and purses. Her eyes widened and she looked to Jeb self-consciously, only to find him with his own book. "We can share," he offered. Reluctantly, she nodded and they shared the small book, about the size of his hand, and they stood to sing. Her voice was rusty and she couldn't recall the last time she had sung anything, but everyone sang with gusto whether they matched the tune or not, and it was a joyful noise.

The pastor started into his sermon after they'd sung two more hymns. "Charity. What is it? Why does it matter?"

He looked over the congregation as he waited for them to think about his questions and how they might answer if they were called to do so.

"Charity is in it's simplest form the love and care we give our fellow men and women. People who need help. People who don't."

There were nods from several men and women in the congregation. Rowena looked sideways at Jeb to see if he was nodding. He was listening, but not nodding. He sat still with his focus fully on the pastor.

"Charity matters because it's one of the ways we have to show the true love of Christ," the pastor continued. He took out his Bible and opened it reverently. "Turn with me if you will to Matthew. Chapter Twenty-five. Let's start with verse thirty-five. 'For I was hungry and you gave me something to eat, I was thirsty and you gave me something to drink, I was a stranger and you invited me in, I needed clothes and you clothed me, I was sick and you looked after me, I was in prison and you came to visit me.'"

Rowena was listening to the words from the Bible and she became enthralled in the words. Captivated at the beauty of a command to help others. She unexpectedly realized that she wanted to help others. For so long she'd been the one in need and others had reached out to help her at times. She was grateful as she looked back.

"And then in verse forty we read… Truly, I say to you, as you did it to one of the least of these my brothers, you did it to me. So my friends, the Bible tells us that we show the Lord to others when we minister to their needs. We're called by God to do that. We're obligated to help those in need."

Rowena continued to drink the words in. Things were making sense in just a few words from a man she'd never met. She wanted to know more.

The pastor read more scripture with spirit and strength as he stood behind the pulpit before them, waving his arms at times as though his message was a new and exciting revelation. And to Rowena, it was. Everything that came from his mouth was fascinating, and she found herself on the edge of her seat, listening curiously. She was nearly disappointed when the service came to a close, and they sang their final hymn.

Her heart pounded in her chest as though it were trying to escape. Trying to control herself, Rowena kept her head down as she followed Jeb out of the bustling chapel as everyone began to greet one another. There were two people who called out to Jeb, but he just tipped his hat and kept walking.

They were on their way back to the Jessup home when she could hold it in no longer. "That was lovely!" she proclaimed, much louder than she had planned. Inhaling sharply, Rowena bit her tongue and looked down. "I mean, I thought that went very well. The service and all."

The man was grinning at her, she could feel it. "Yes, I… I thought so, too. You liked it, then?" She nodded enthusiastically. "You should come more often," he told

her. "It's every Sunday, after all," and he said it teasingly, like they were joking.

Flushed, Rowena's beating heart gave her the courage to meet his gaze. "I just might," she nodded. "I want
to, really. Why, I've never been...well, I've never been
to church before now," the young woman confessed,
not sure why she was saying this. "In New York, my
life never warranted it. I'd hardly been inside a chapel
before, and the pastors I heard of only yelled and told
us how we were all going to Hell." She paused, frowning. "Is it always like this, or does he do some shouting, as well?"

Jeb shook his head, to her relief. "Pastor Simmons
is as nice as they come. I guess he might get spirited
from time to time, but I don't think he shouts much."

Feeling reassured, Rowena smiled. And they started
into a stumbling discussion over what they had heard
that day, as she gathered her courage to ask him questions and he stammered his way through answers.

They were at the house before she knew it, and she
frowned. Jeb was still talking as he leaped down and
hurried over to help her back onto the ground. As she
climbed off the wagon, Susannah appeared in the doorway and waved. They were still a few yards off, but the
short woman had a loud voice.

"About time you two returned! Come and eat!"

Rowena paused, and weighed her options as Jeb
turned to her with a sheepish grin. "Well, we can always finish this discussion next time," he offered her.
"I'd definitely like to see what you, um, what you think
of the story about Jonah and the big fish."

She raised an eyebrow. "Big fish?"

"It's got a lot to do with faith," he assured her. "The Jessups can tell you where to find it in their Bible."

Chewing on the inside of her cheek, Rowena nodded and grudgingly stepped back. She glanced at the house, and then a thought came to mind that she found herself impulsively voicing. "Or you can come in and tell me about it," she invited him. "I'm sure she meant for both of us to come in and eat, after all."

He pulled off his hat, squinting at her in the sunlight. His brown hair appeared to turn a soft gold just then, and it only accented his grin all the more. "That would be mighty nice," he ventured. "I'd like that. Let me take care of the horse and I'll be right in."

"Of course." She nodded, and dropped her gaze. "Then I'll—we'll—see you inside."

Chapter Fourteen

Jeb joined the ladies for the noonday meal that Sunday, and left shortly afterwards to join Lucas in town. They had an enlightening conversation about the Holy Bible and the pastor and Rowena spent the better part of the next week reading.

She didn't see Jeb again until he showed up the next Sunday morning with the wagon to take her to church. It was unexpected, but she couldn't deny a sliver of hope that had been shining in her heart.

"What do you think today's sermon will be about?" She invited discussion on the drive over, noticing that he was waiting for her to take the lead.

He grinned. "Probably about hard work and laboring in the Lord's vineyard. He likes to talk about that in spring and summer. You know, to um, prepare everyone for planting and harvest."

She looked at him carefully, trying to decide if he was joking or not. "Oh really?"

"Or he'll talk about Jonah and the big fish," he shrugged.

Now she knew it. Straightening up, she wrinkled her nose at him, not sure how she felt about this. "Hmm." After a minute of musing, her thoughts had already wandered. "Do they sing the same songs every week?"

They talked on the way over, and again shared his hymn book. On the drive back, she looked through it and mused over the songs. Rowena hadn't grown up around that much music, though she'd heard plenty in the streets. There was always music in the gambling house, but that was much different.

Over the following month, it became a tradition and Rowena found herself looking forward to her Sundays in church. The songs were always filled with joy, and the sermons taught about forgiveness, trust, and grace. It was a world she had never known, and found herself craving more of. During most of her free time, she'd find a cozy spot and open the Holy Bible to read.

"We're heading into town in a few minutes," Susannah called to her from the kitchen. "Lucas needs to take care of his paperwork, and there are errands to run. Would you like to join us?"

Glancing up from the book, Rowena wiggled in her chair by the window and considered it. She was at the story of King David, and was wondering if she wanted to find out the ending now, or wait. Biting her lip, she glanced at the book and then back to Susannah.

"It will still be here when we return," she promised.

Chuckling, Rowena nodded. "All right, then. Do we need to bring anything more?" Putting the book down, she went over to the kitchen to see the three boxes sitting on the table, all filled with freshly pulled carrots they had pulled out of their garden yesterday. "There we are," she had her question answered for her as Susannah chuckled and took out a box to the wagon Lucas was setting up for them.

Soon they were on their way, and Rowena was helping Susannah unload the boxes at the mercantile. The older woman fell into conversation with the shop owner, Mr. Dowdle, and soon the work was done but the talking wasn't. Rowena had little to say about the coming harvest, so she wandered the aisles of the shop and then went to stand out on the porch, trying to distract herself.

"Miss Oakton?"

She turned to find Jeb strolling down the street. Pulling off his hat, he grinned and hastened over. "Good afternoon, Mr. Harbin." She nodded and offered him a smile. "What are you doing here?"

"Please, I think we're past niceties." He shook his head. "Call me Jeb. And I should ask you the same thing. Rocky Ridge only sees you in town on Sundays, after all. Would you like to join me for lunch? I'm headed down to the restaurant."

Biting her lip, she squinted up at the sun shining down on them. It was a warm day, and she felt a fine line of sweat beginning to break out on her forehead. She had forgotten her bonnet, and knew she would be dark before the day was out. Shrugging it off, Rowena turned to find Susannah, and waved to get her attention.

The woman noticed, and saw Jeb there. Her eyes widened in understanding and she gestured, showing that it was all right for her to go. Susannah returned to her conversation with Mr. Dowdle and Rowena found herself walking down the street with Jeb.

It was a comfortable position, she realized, as he

started talking about his day, the way they walked to-gether. The two of them were close but not touching. When necessary, he offered his hand and she would take it then and only then. Granted, this was different to be walking and talking away from the chapel and the Jessup house.

She noticed people watching them, probably asking each other who she was. After all, they had to know Jeb. But the stares made her uneasy and it reminded her of the gambling house, of the men lurking in the shad-ows and watching every move. Why did people need to be so nosey?

"Here we are," Jeb opened the door for her, and she stepped in. It was a cozy place, and already bustling with people sitting in their seats and a few walking around. The lights were dim compared to the sun and it took her a minute for her eyes to adjust. By then, Jeb had already spotted a table for them, and guided her around to the corner. He pulled out her chair, and sat across from her.

"You come here often, don't you?" Rowena asked as she carefully glanced around the room. Most of the people there looked over and waved. Her lunch partner was more than kind to wave back, and offer greetings. For a moment, she nearly felt ignored.

Jeb shook his head. "It's a small town, so people know me, I suppose." He offered her one of those grins again, and was about to say something else when some-one hollered at him.

"About time you was here, Jeb! Your bacon is burn-ing. Same thing again?"

Laughing, he looked at Rowena apologetically before shouting his own response. "Same thing again."

"And how's about that lady friend of yours?"

He sputtered for a moment before clearing his throat. "I uh, I'm sorry about this, Miss Oakton. But um, what would you like? You're hungry, aren't you?"

Her face flushed and she shook her head. "Oh no, please don't bother for me. Susannah brought a basket."

Jeb shrugged. "Please, I'm the one who—who dragged you away. The least I can do is provide you a decent meal in return for your company. You mentioned you like ham, I believe?"

"Yes," she nodded reluctantly. Biting her lip, Rowena stared at the wooden table, not sure how to handle this situation. There had been a time when she was struggling to survive off the streets after leaving that gambling house. Even though Susannah and Lucas fed her, it was strange to be out and about around the town and having someone else pay for her. Especially a gentleman.

"She'll have the same. No bacon, just the ham," he called back. "Her name is Rowena Oakton."

Her eyes widened and she gave him a look. Everyone was clearly paying attention to this, even if there were other conversations still going on. "Please, I don't…" She trailed off hesitantly, not even sure what she wanted to say.

"Welcome, Miss Rowena Oakton!" The voice called back. "I'm Sam, the cook. It's a pleasure to have you here!"

Freezing, she glanced around but it was like a voice in the void, and she couldn't see where he was. Rowena looked at Jeb helplessly who shrugged with that grin of his. "Thank you, Sam!" She finally shouted back, and she could have sworn she heard someone cheer. Shaking her head, she tried to make herself small again to avoid the embarrassment. "Is it always like this?"

Jeb chuckled. "I'm afraid so. I'm sorry about that. Sam's real friendly. He's real nice, but he can't have quiet conversations since he's in the kitchen. This is his place, you see, and uh, I guess I do come here often. I'm not as good a cook as he is, after all."

Finding the strength to laugh it off, Rowena watched as Jeb's confidence grew and hers seemed to disappear. She was nervous and quiet as they ate, still trying to process in her mind what they were even doing.

As the days passed, however, she thought more about Jeb and realized they had developed a friendship. Jeb was humorous and kind, and hopeful about the future in a way that Rowena had never experienced. He wanted to learn as much as he could to build a good life for himself, and she admired that. All she had ever focused on was survival. It's how she was raised and it was all she'd ever known. Until now.

When Jeb wasn't working in town or on his house, he started dropping by the Jessup house. He ended up teaching Rowena to ride, and they discussed the Gospel in the evenings. Susannah and Lucas were around intermittently, and the young woman was glad for it. She liked knowing she had support when she needed it, but she also liked the space since she hadn't yet recovered her complete trust in them.

But Jeb was a good distraction. She quickly learned that he did have a devilish side to him, having grown up around other rowdy boys and then having joined the Rangers. Most of his stories were about practical jokes and stunts he had narrowly escaped, so Rowena learned to laugh out loud. That grin did his stories justice, she decided, even if the man was shy around her.

He treated her so respectfully, that Rowena almost didn't know what to do. As their friendship developed, she began wondering if she did want him walking closer to her, maybe bumping shoulders. Or if their hands touched while sharing the hymn book, she wondered why she wasn't afraid. Rowena couldn't get any further than that, however, because it always brought back memories of the gambling house. She remembered the roving eyes, the prodding fingers and grabbing hands.

He was a good man, Rowena knew, but just how good? She shuddered at the thought of being wrong.

Chapter Fifteen

It was a beautiful day, Susannah sighed. She looked about the porch as she hemmed one of Lucas's shirts. The sky was blue with few clouds hanging around, and it was just warm enough that the shade kept her cool. Nimbly her fingers wound around the fabric, and she cut the thread with her teeth.

Satisfied, she turned to the socks. She was in the middle of the second when she glanced up again and found Rowena and Jeb coming over the hill. Her eyes focused on the couple. They looked good together, she acknowledged, from their skin tone to their smiles, they matched. Maybe she would be good at this matchmaking thing after all. Granted, this wasn't the way she had intended to begin the whole business. But if this one worked, then Susannah had a feeling that things would go more smoothly the next time.

After all, what was she to do? Rowena had clearly arrived on their doorstep without a plan, without knowing what she was doing with her life. The young woman needed a purpose, and she needed to be kept busy. The first few months were focused on learning new skills, on adapting to her new living space.

But she couldn't stay here forever, and she had to know that. Rowena Oakton was a lovely young lady, but the west was hardly the place for a woman on her own. And that was a fact, Susannah acknowledged, one they had to accept whether they liked it or not. What better way then, to find a good man? She had come to the right place.

Susannah grinned as Jeb reached out and helped Rowena who stumbled on the path. It was coming together quite nicely, she decided. The idea had only been half-baked, but it was coming together more and more each day. The idea of Jeb inviting her to church had been inspired by Lucas, who had noticed Rowena's uncomfortable demeanor when they talked about the Bible or church. He wondered if the concept was new to her.

After that, the meetings had been more than easy enough to arrange. The young man simply started coming around more often, and it only took her a little convincing to talk Lucas into having Jeb turn up when they were in town. Matchmaking was fun, Susannah discovered, and it made her feel so good to be helping others.

As the couple drew closer, Susannah recalled how she had started setting everything up for the Boarding House business. As she had mentioned it to her closest friends, they shared the news around town quietly but surely. Word was getting around, for those closest to her in Rocky Ridge, some even as far as Colorado Springs, began coming to visit.

She had spent enough time talking to each of the men. So far, she had six lined up for those that she had thoroughly interviewed, checked on their references, and compiled a portfolio on them. Already there were two young women headed west in a few months and this would really put things to the test.

They were supposed to be the first, but then Rowena showed up and Susannah couldn't turn her away. Jeb Harbin was a good man, a young man with a good job starting out in his life. He'd come to Rocky Ridge to leave the Texas Rangers as her husband had done. Susannah supposed it was the similarities that kept him on her mind, and she had started seeing what she could do for him. For him and for Rowena.

"There you two are." Susannah beamed at them as they finally reached the porch. "Is that what I think it is?"

Rowena nodded, pulling back the towel covering the basket. "Plenty to make a nice batch of preserves, I believe."

"Maybe two batches," Jeb said. "We found a big patch of wild strawberries and picked every ripe one we could find."

"With a few flowers," the girl continued, bringing forth a few sunflowers they had put on top. "Aren't they lovely? They're so big!" She looked up at Jeb who grinned back at her, as though this were a private joke. Susannah's smile stretched wide across her face, watching the two of them. "I'll go take care of these," Rowena assured her, and slipped right into the kitchen.

Her eyes followed the girl until she was far enough inside that she wouldn't hear anything. Still smiling, Susannah set her pile of clothes to one side, and waved

Jeb over to her. The man pulled off his hat and took a deep breath as he sat on the bench to her left.

"It looks like things between you and Rowena are going well," she said, inviting discussion. Trying to read his few expressions, Susannah put down the needle. "What do you think of her?"

At the mention of her name, Jeb's cheek twitched. Looking at the ground, his shoulders relaxed and she saw the smile he was trying to suppress. "She's lovely," he said finally. "A real lady."

"She is," Susannah chuckled. "That she is. I'm sorry to intrude on your thoughts, but it would help me to understand as much as possible. What do you like about her most? You had very little to say before about your preferences in your portfolio, after all. I believe your only requests were for someone happy, and someone skilled within the home setting?"

Nodding, he played with the brim of his hat. The man looked nice today, as he always did lately now that Rowena was in the picture. Upon his arrival to Rocky Ridge, Jeb had looked more like a boy playing in the mud with his rundown clothes and that sloppy grin. He'd stayed in their barn a few nights before finding a spot of land he'd spent months camping on until starting to build his house. It was slow going at first since he had little interest in it.

But since he had come to her to start on his profile and with the idea of a possible family in the future, Jeb had grown determined to start growing and working on his homestead. Lucas, who had worked with him as Rangers, said he had completely changed from the rowdy young man he had been.

The shyness factor, however, still remained and Jeb hardly met her gaze. "That's right, yes. I… I mean, other traits are always good as well, but I wasn't even sure what I wanted. I guess I wasn't completely sure about what I'm supposed to want. But now that I've met her—" Jeb took a deep breath "—she's exactly what I want and more. She's clever and smart, and talented. Rowena is…" but he didn't know how to finish it.

It was good enough of an answer. Susannah noted the words in her mind so that she could write them down later. "Good," she said after a moment. "She really is lovely, and I do love having her around. Now, is there anything that has gone wrong, anything we should be changing? Are you comfortable? Is there anything wrong?"

After all, she had noticed the space between them. Jeb was a gentleman, always willing to share an arm or helping hand. But Rowena rarely took it, and hardly touched him. They walked side by side but never touched, and that concerned Susannah. Obviously it had to be a pressure point.

But the look he gave her said otherwise. Flitting his gaze between her and the door, Jeb shook his head. "She should know. I understand you thought it best not to mention it until she was comfortable here, but…we're beyond that. I don't want to start a relationship of any kind based on mistrust."

He looked at the ground, but seemed set on his thought.

Susannah sighed. This wasn't a subject she wanted to tackle with Rowena. She was fairly certain the girl had forgiven her for not being completely honest in the ad she placed, but she knew trust was still a problem.

"That's no way to live. I learned that in the Rangers, ma'am, you always need to be able to trust your partners. If you can't, then you won't survive. She's playing a part she doesn't know about, and I don't feel comfortable with that."

He looked up and his gaze pierced hers and Susannah looked away, feeling troubled about this as well. It had appeared easy enough in the beginning, that things would fix themselves and work out perfectly. But there was a chance, she knew in her heart, that this had gone too far and now it might cause more damage than good. If Rowena found out now, what would she think? There was so much that the young woman never said, never talked about.

"I know," Susannah acknowledged this at last. "I know." Sighing, she shook her head. "I do need to talk to her. This isn't your fault, Jeb, please know that. I was impulsive. I will try to find the best way to talk her."

"Soon?"

The door opened and Jeb hurriedly stood as Rowena appeared in the doorway. She eyed them warily as the party of two smiled at her. Susannah's heart beat quickly, wondering if she had heard something.

Finally, the young woman smiled back and brought out a mug of lemonade for Jeb. "I thought you might be thirsty. You said you needed to be getting back to town, but I didn't want you going back without a drink."

"Thank you," Jeb nodded. "Would you walk with me to my horse?"

She acquiesced and started down the stairs. Jeb

glanced back as he followed after her, catching Susannah's eye with a questioning gaze. She gave him a resolute nod, a silent promise, and then she watched them walk away. Taking a deep breath, she prayed for forgiveness with the hope that things would turn out for the better.

Chapter Sixteen

The moment Jeb was trotting away on his brown shaggy horse, Rowena glanced back at the house only to start off in her own direction. Susannah was still sitting on the porch with her needle and thread, but the idea of stepping near that woman shook Rowena to her bones.

It had only been a doubt, a small thought she had harbored and tried to ignore. But she had heard enough, and her hands were still shaking. Hiking up the hills, the young woman glanced down at her hands and balled them into fists. Frowning, she put them away and marched faster. The forceful steps allowed her to focus on expending her energies through physical motions, distracting her from her thoughts. This worked all the way until she reached the top of the hill.

Her chest heaving for breath, she paused to rest on her knees. Squeezing her eyes tight, Rowena inhaled deeply and leaned against a large tree trunk. The quaking within her heart lessened with the pressure in her lungs. In a way, this was better, she decided. For a minute she could ignore the nerves building up within her that were so anxious to escape.

One deep breath, and another. Number three, four, and five more before she felt composed enough to straighten up. Stretching, Rowena gulped and glanced around at the scenery. Though she still had to be on the Jessup property, she was higher than she had ever been before. It was dizzying, the height at which she stood with the world below. There were higher mountains around her, but she couldn't imagine climbing any higher.

Jeb had said he had taken on taller mountains further west. But she shook her head. She didn't want him on her mind right now. She didn't want anyone on her mind. She wanted to be alone, to think clearly. Heart beating, blood rushing, Rowena looked around her as she thought things out.

An eagle soared above, calling out as he passed over her. He was free, flying wherever he wished. Rowena leaned against the tree and glanced up. What she wouldn't give to be like that, to be so independent and rely on no one. All she wanted was the chance to be herself, and stop worrying about what would happen if she was able to be on her own. The future was unpredictable enough, and to leave it up to someone else was far from reassuring.

All her life, she could not recall the parents who had given her birth and who had passed away too early to give her a childhood. A concept that had never existed for Rowena for she had been raised in a run-down shack with her aunt and uncle. They were heavy drinkers with loose morals and heavy fists. The moment she was old enough, they sent her to the factories where she was worked to exhaustion.

When she wound up at the gambling house, she thought it was a stroke of good luck. Rowena spent two years giving her best in the quiet of the early mornings, cleaning up after it closed. But then they noticed her looks and put her out on the gambling house floors where she was exploited and used. She received more social interaction than she'd ever experienced or ever wanted.

Once she had run off and lived on the streets, only then had she been able to go where she wanted and do whatever she wanted on her own. Clearly it wasn't the best decision or way she had survived thus far, but at least there had been no one to answer to, no one telling her what to do.

Staring at her hands, Rowena wondered why this only appeared to happen to her, if she was just that cursed. Why was it so difficult to find any peace? Even now she was much too anxious to enjoy the wondrous sight before her. It was spectacular, she acknowledged that, but her thoughts were too mixed up and she couldn't appreciate the surroundings with so much going on in her heart and mind.

"Maybe I'm just imagining it," she murmured, twisting her hands absently. "That's not what they meant, I'm making things up. They're friends, that's all they are. They aren't really..." but her breath caught and she couldn't continue the sentence.

A lump formed in her throat and Rowena rubbed her face as though it would clear her mind. If what she had managed to understand from the conversation on the porch was real, then it was a plot. But if she'd heard wrong, she tried to reason, then she was being foolish.

So she needed proof, that's what she needed.

Gathering herself, Rowena managed a few more deep breaths so that her heart might slow down to its normal pace once again. Only then did she straighten herself up and once composed, started back down the hill.

"There you are." Susannah peeked her head out from the kitchen and waved a towel. "I was wondering where you had wandered off to. Is everything all right? You look tired."

Self-consciously Rowena glanced down at her dirty dress. It had been the nicer one, and now it was worse than her other gown. Shrugging it off, she offered a tight smile. "Everything's fine. And you're right, I am tired. I think I'll retire for the evening, if you don't mind?"

"Of course." Susannah nodded hurriedly. "Do let me know if you need anything."

Rowena nodded and headed off. She was halfway to her room and passing the bookcase in the main room when she decided to pause and glance in, seeing the sunlight through the window. The room fascinated her, since one of the mill workers, an old Irish man by the name of Grady, had taken pity on her and taught her to read during the long hours of feeding metal onto the conveyor belts. Usually she focused on the Holy Bible, but occasionally she'd come through here and choose one of the books, and just sit among the pages.

It was a nice, cozy room, after all. She sat down at the small desk, enjoying the feel of the smooth leather and cheery oak. The Jessups hardly used the piece of furniture, except for Susannah who could occasionally be seen there, working on pieces of paper. Shuffled pages organized into files that had to be kept somewhere and clearly meant something to her. Biting her lip, Rowena considered where they could be.

Keeping an eye on the cracked open door where Susannah could enter at any time, Rowena began digging. Hurriedly and quietly, she nimbly looked through the various papers in the drawers until finally, she found it.

They weren't hard to find. But they were hard to swallow. A lump formed in her throat as she found the name at the very top of the pile. Rowena ran her fingers over the brown cover and took a shaky breath. His name was right there, mocking her.

"Jeb," she whispered, a quiet moan that betrayed more emotion than she had comprehended. But she pushed it down, and left it behind as she forced herself to read.

The first page covered the basics, about the man himself. She skimmed the page, reviewing much of what she already knew. It expounded upon his childhood, his education, and his work experience. The following pages were what appeared to be letters of reference by people she didn't know. Glancing anxiously towards the door, Rowena continued to read.

He has saved my neck a number of times...a good man in time of need...quiet until you know him...a sense of humor like no other...

She skimmed their words thoughtfully.

And then came the real treat, that of Susannah's insights. Not just of Jeb, however, but of herself. The moment she saw her name, she stood and the chair squealed as it moved backwards. She bit her lip and froze finally, waiting for the footsteps she was certain would come.

They didn't.

Still, she knew her time was limited. Sucking in a deep breath, she held the pages in her hands and couldn't decide what to do. Did she want to read it? Rowena wasn't certain she wanted to know what Susannah thought of her. Already she knew too much. Susannah had continued with her little game, roping her into this scheme without her awareness or desire to be part of it.

And Jeb had gone along with it. That, or perhaps he had even conspired to begin it. His devilish grin told the truth now, this entire setup. Rowena could feel the panic rising within her. It itched beneath the skin, tickling her spine. She wanted to claw it out, but didn't know how. Only by leaving could she escape this manipulation. They hadn't said a single thing to her but considered her a pawn. She had to take herself out of the plan. Now.

She scrambled about, putting away the papers. She had seen enough. With shaking hands, Rowena put the desk back the way it was and went to the door. She was just stepping out when a shadow came before her and she jumped.

"Ah." Lucas was there, his closed expression staring her down. In the dim lighting, the scar on the side of his face gave him a menacing look. Though she had seen the way he was with Susannah, the way he acted as a gentleman at all times, Rowena knew he was a good man. But all the same, he was an unsettling figure with a rugged past and she was already on edge.

He didn't even react when she jumped. The man

merely stepped back and nodded. "I apologize. I should have had a light in the hallway."

Clenching her jaw, she shook her head. "No, that's all right. I... I wasn't expecting anyone, that's all. Pardon me," Rowena added and stepped around him.

"Will you be joining us for supper? Or do you have other plans?"

She froze. If he mentioned it to Susannah, then the woman would know she hadn't turned in yet. And then she would know something was up. Heart hammering, Rowena swallowed. "I'm afraid not. I was... I just wanted to put a book away. I had it out earlier, you see, and I...well, my head aches. So I wanted to rest now."

"Of course," the man said finally. "Good night, then, Miss Oakton."

"Good night." She hurried off, for she had much to do, and it was late.

Chapter Seventeen

It was only a small cottage with two rooms. With dark wood, the windows were just barely set in with painted shutters. A small dirt path led the way from the road, an outline of rocks to keep the weeds out. There was a backdrop of hills behind the home, so it was a breathtaking view from anywhere within the house. The back door had a porch, one that he wanted to expand.

There was a lot he wanted to do, Jeb reminded himself. A never-ending project, there was much to be accomplished to consider his home and land completed. And even then, there was constant upkeep and farming once he reached that point. Life was a project filled with tasks in between, with plenty of ways to be kept busy in order to keep surviving.

Sometimes it was a lot of fun, he admitted, thinking of the good times. It was worth it, between all the complications and trials. Though it had been a hard life, he had plenty of good times with good company. Jeb's thoughts wandered through many memories, until it moved towards the present, and she came to mind.

Rowena Oakton was a beautiful young woman, clever and exciting to be around. Just the thought of her made his cheeks flush and his hands clammy. He closed his eyes, and could picture her there beside him in the house. The way she laughed, throwing back her head with those bright eyes. Even how she walked beside him, close and comfortable as though they had been doing this for years.

Watching her come to love the Bible and God's teachings had been a joy he'd never experienced. Being able to be part of her new understanding and grow with her had been inspiring and it had refreshed his own beliefs.

His eyes opened and he looked around. And Jeb frowned, realizing she wasn't around. It was in that moment then, he realized how much he missed her when she wasn't around, and how much he wished she was there. That she was here, for all of this. He realized then that he wanted her there, for always.

Biting the inside of his cheek, he tried to imagine asking for her hand in marriage. Would she accept him? He stood up and began to pace. He felt restless as he pondered the question.

Lately she walked closer to him with their elbows occasionally brushing against one another. When they sat together in church, there was hardly an inch of space between them. Every part of him said that she was the one who he wanted to settle down with. Except there might be one little problem.

Recalling his conversation with Susannah Jessup, he shook his head and dropped back into his chair. Looking up at the ceiling, he knew couldn't do anything until he told Rowena what was going on. He couldn't lie like this anymore, he couldn't be dishonest about the way this had been initiated. It would be a relationship founded on a lie, on a scheme, and he couldn't do that to her. And just as importantly, he didn't want to risk losing her or her trust later if she found out.

The guilt had been gnawing at him since he found out Rowena wasn't aware of Susannah's plan. She deserved the truth. Shaking his head, he tried to figure this out. How would he tell her? He jumped up and began to pace again. He spent the evening trying to find the right words to say.

He hardly slept the night through, and rushed to get ready for the day. After cutting himself twice while shaving, Jeb hastily dressed and headed towards the Jessup's home—and Rowena.

"Good morning." Susannah offered a questioning smile when she opened the door. "Jeb, I wasn't—we weren't expecting you this early. Were we?"

Shaking his head, he stepped through the doorway and looked around doggedly. "Good morning. Yes, that is—I mean, no, I… Is Rowena around? I'd like to speak with her." He turned and met the woman's gaze with determination. "I'm going to tell her the truth."

Her lips parted in surprise before she shook her head. "Now, Jeb, I'm not sure—"

"Where is she?" He couldn't contain his impatience, though he felt bad for his rudeness. Frowning, Jeb headed into the kitchen with Susannah following right behind. "I can't do this to her any longer, ma'am, I'm sorry." When Rowena wasn't found around here, they headed towards her room.

He knocked on the door twice, and another when

there was no answer. Brow furrowed, he looked at Susannah who shrugged. She looked as confused as he
was. "I swear I haven't heard her today," she murmured
to herself, and opened the door a crack. "Rowena? Are
you awake? Is everything all right?" She peeked her
head in only a little, until finally she opened the door
completely.

The room was clean and the bed was made. In fact, it
was too clean. Frowning, Jeb glanced around and wondered what was wrong with this. Susannah stepped into
the room, clutching the towel to her chest. She turned
in a circle with darting eyes, biting her lip. After a moment, she hiccupped and looked at him, fear in her eyes.

"What's wrong?" he demanded.

"She's gone," Susannah whispered. "All of her
things, gone. I don't…what happened?" But neither
of them knew the answer. The woman frantically ran
around the room, looking through the blankets and
closet trying to find something she might have left behind. Maybe a clue or something. "Oh, no. I can't believe she did this."

He swallowed hard, bracing himself. Her room
looked as though it had never been slept in. Clearly
Rowena wanted to make it appear as though she had
never been there. Frowning, he shook his head. He'd
been trained to deal with difficult situations with little
or nothing to go on. The young woman had left by her
own decision, gone without a word. Jeb knew that much.

He knew Rowena liked it here, but there was much
of her past he didn't know. He knew she had fears and
had faced trials she had yet to share.

"I can't believe it," Susannah was moaning. "We

should have told her. I know she heard us, I'm certain of it now. What was I thinking? No one should treat a girl like that the way I have. You were right, Jeb. What have I done?"

Her words made everything click. As bold as Rowena tried to be, if she had heard, if she already knew… his breath caught and he couldn't imagine the state the young woman would be in. If that's how she found out, anyway.

Without another word, Jeb turned and ran to the door. Susannah was in a state, but nothing could be done until Rowena was found. But where was she? Leaving behind his jacket and hat, he returned to his horse left saddled by the front gate and left at a gallop.

The sun was bright as he gripped the reins and kept an eagle eye out for the world around him. Where would she have gone? Did she even know where she was going? Then it hit him like a bolt of lightning, and he pulled his horse to an immediate halt. He was letting his feelings drive his actions. Foolish!

After spending years as a Texas Ranger, he had developed more than decent tracking skills. Turning his horse around, Jeb returned to the Jessup house, and started looking for tracks or anything that might be a clue for the direction she'd gone. It was nearly impossible to find a particular set since everyone walked around there all day long. He found several tracks and wandered around the garden and barn before he finally found something. There was a set of tracks that looked fresh leading down the road.

Now, he went carefully, riding his horse down the trail. Looking as he went, Jeb tracked the trail all the way into town. It was nearly noon by then, and Rocky Ridge was bustling. The hope he'd been gathering in his heart faded away as he looked at the busy streets. There was no chance of finding her here, not now.

Driving his horse through town, Jeb wandered the streets over and over, going in circles until he thought he was going to lose his mind. The best tracker on his team, he'd never failed to find what he was looking for. In this case, he cared more than ever about what happened next. Jumping off his horse, Jeb ran into the restaurant, hoping to find her there.

Perhaps she had stopped for something to eat. Sam called out to him, but Jeb didn't hear as he skimmed the room once, twice, three times before he turned and ran out into the road. Deciding she might have headed to the hotel in town, he went there but Mr. Childers promised she hadn't been there.

He kicked a post in his frustration. Limping back into the street, Jeb groaned in frustration and started off for his horse. Having left the animal tied to a post, he tried to consider if he was missing something. If she had heard about being wrapped up in the scheme, Jeb told himself, she would have left. She despised lies and desired her independence.

She would be alone. She'd be on foot with her few possessions in a bag since she didn't own a horse. He hadn't checked to make sure she hadn't taken a horse from the Jessup's barn, but he knew she would never have done that. Plus her footprints going away from the property supported what his heart knew about her integrity.

She would have slipped out very early for the Jessups not to have noticed. Clearly she had headed into town, the only other place she knew. Where would she go next?

"Hi, Mr. Harbin," the children chimed as he passed by.

Absently he waved, too distracted to help them jump rope or play with their hoops. Usually he had free time to teach them tricks and chase them around, but he couldn't think of anything else right now. He needed to focus on finding Rowena, on finding someone who could help him. But then something came to mind.

Searching the children's faces, he looked for the right one. Playing hopscotch with her friends was the Childers' daughter, Penny, and Jeb hurried over. If anyone was to have recognized Rowena in town, it would be Penny, for her family sat two rows behind them every Sunday.

"Miss Penny! Do you have a moment?" The girl hopped over. Crouching down to her level, he looked at the young girl with a loud voice who had too much energy for her overworked parents. Trying to smile, Jeb took a deep breath. "I'm in a hurry, and I can't find my friend. Do you remember the girl…the young lady I sit with in church? With the pretty brown hair like yours?"

Petting her hair, the young girl nodded. "Yep, Momma said she came out of nowhere to Rocky Ridge. Father said her name is pretty, but I don't remember what it was. Why do you sit with her?"

Jeb could feel his cheeks heating up and he ruffled his hair. "Well, because I think she's pretty, and I like her. But Penny, I can't find her."

The young girl giggled. "Are you playing hide and seek?"

For a moment, words failed him. "Yes," he said finally. "Yes, and I've definitely lost in the game. But I need to find her to talk to her. Have you seen her?"

Penny looked around carefully and then nodded several times. She leaned over and put a hand to her mouth to hide her words in a whisper. "I saw her this morning. She was going to the train station."

Jeb started, and stood to go. "You're certain?"

The girl gave him a look similar to that of any woman whenever she was questioned about what she knew. Penny's lips pursed as she crossed her arms and Jeb stepped back with his hands up in defense. "You're not very good at this game."

"I know." He nodded and stood up. "Thank you, Penny! You're a sweet girl to help."

Jeb left his horse and the children behind, running down the street. The station was only a few blocks down. Then he stumbled, recalling the train schedule. On Mondays there were only two trains that passed through, and the first one was due just about now. Had he missed it? Jeb glanced at the sun and prayed that it wasn't too late.

Chapter Eighteen

She was hot, anxious, and exhausted. Rowena looked around the train depot impatiently, clutching her bag tightly. Her worn down boots were rubbing her heels painfully as she stood leaning against a wall. The sight around her was far from favorable, and she wasn't in the mood for any more trouble.

After yesterday's discovery, she hadn't been able to sleep. Though she had attempted to rest for a few hours, she was only in bed until she was certain that the Jessup couple was down for the night. Once the house was quiet, Rowena had finished cleaning her room and left the house. Knowing it would take time to walk the several miles into town, she spent all morning walking on the dusty road, determined to find her freedom one way or another. On her own.

And now, hours later, here she was. Standing alone in the crowd, trying to blend in. She hadn't had enough money to buy a ticket on the first train out of town, but the clerk had mercy on her. He'd given her a pass to ride to Denver.

Her hope was simple. That the God she now trusted would look after her. That He would provide a job and a place to stay when she got to Denver. Maybe Denver would become her home.

The paper with the note from the clerk weighed in her pocket. Her heart was so heavy about leaving a place she'd come to love, but the sense of betrayal by people she also had come to love was too much. The pass to get on the train signified another new start.

Yet the train was late. She hadn't been positive on the time, but the other folks waiting to board were just as antsy as she was. Rowena listened to the chatter, only growing more jittery as the time went by. What if it never came? If it didn't come soon, she knew she would lose her nerve.

She had wanted to turn back several times. Just the thought of the kind faces of Susannah and Lucas and Jeb made her throat close up. As much as they might have toyed with her, they had still treated her with more kindness than she had ever experienced before. Would she be able to find something like that again? Were there other people out in the world who were truly kind and caring?

They had given her so much. And now she was leaving them, without a proper farewell. Her heart dropped and she sniffled. But then Rowena stomped her foot, gathering her resolve again. Ignoring the looks, she took a deep breath and reminded herself that she had been lied to, and what they had done was a cruel trick.

"Rowena!" So lost in her thoughts, she didn't hear her name being called at first. "Rowena Oakton!" Only when a hand brushed against her elbow did Rowena jump, gasping when she noticed Jeb in front of her. Her eyes widened.

Jeb was covered in dust, his clothes a mess and his hair ruffled. His face had two small cuts and one had a bit of blood around it. She wasn't sure why she even noticed the cuts, but something made her notice everything since this might be the last time she saw him.

Panting, he bent over to catch his breath. He tried to talk, but the stammering and dust in his mouth stopped her from understanding anything he said. Stunned, she didn't know what to do, so she pulled her bag closer to her chest, pressing herself against the wall.

People were staring at them, and her cheeks heated up in embarrassment. Swallowing, she glanced towards the tracks again, wondering where the train was. Then she glanced back at Jeb who was coughing now. Fighting the urge to run away from him, something kept her from leaving his side. Biting her lip, she hesitantly patted his back. "Are you all right?"

"No," he wheezed. "Not until—at least until I—I can talk to you. I have to…have to tell you—all of it. Everything. I have to…tell you."

He wanted to talk? Rowena's heart skipped a beat, but she shook her head. He just wanted to tell her what she already knew, and he was too late for that. Turning back towards the tracks, she started to edge away. But Jeb gulped in a deep breath and straightened up, inadvertently blocking her exit.

"I wanted to tell you all along," Jeb explained, trying to flatten his hair. "But I didn't, I don't know why I didn't. The important thing is that Mrs. Jessup has been helping to set the two of us up, to work on her matchmaking skills for her business. I was already a client, and, well, she—I mean we—thought it might work. With you."

She raised her eyebrow and crossed her arms as he chanced a hesitant glance at her. He had grown comfortable and more confident around her in the last few weeks, but now it was like they had just met again, for he was fumbling over his words and unsure of what to say. Rowena sighed and was about to say something to stop him, but then she heard the far away whistle. The train was coming. She looked up and could see smoke over the ridge.

Turning back to him, Rowena frowned at Jeb. "You're making it sound like it was your idea," she said finally. "And I know it wasn't."

"I just wanted to—you knew?" He stopped short, his eyes widening in surprise. The hope left his gaze, and she saw the pain in his expression. Pain for her? Rowena hesitated, not sure what to think of that.

Swallowing, she nodded. "I overheard the two of you yesterday. And then I found your portfolio. And my name." Rowena pursed her lips and edged around him. "I know it was Susannah's idea, Jeb, you don't need to cover for her. Now excuse me, but I'd like to go now. I want to be in a place where folks won't be playing games with me."

"But where?" Jeb asked her, a heavy emotion weighing within his voice. She paused and looked back at him warily. "Are you going back to New York? Are you leaving us, for good?"

The look in his eye caught her off guard, and Rowena hesitated. She glanced over to the tracks, the train nearly there. Everyone around them was bustling, gathering their packages and preparing to board. Shaking her head, the young woman tried to find the right thing to tell Jeb before she left. But what else could she say? "I don't know," she told him simply. "Just away."

He barred her way again when she tried to step around him. Hands clasped together, Jeb tried to smile but it looked painful. Frowning, Rowena sidestepped in the other direction, but again he was there. Close, nearly touching, and in her way. She groaned in frustration and he winced. "I can't let you go until I talk to you." His stammering had stopped and he sounded sure and resolute.

"What else is there to say?" She stomped her foot. "What? Do you think you can change my mind, or create a different story of what happened? You've already apologized. So that's—"

Jeb interrupted her. "Because you need to know that I care for you. That I truly, deeply, care for you, Rowena, and you deserve to know that above everything else."

Her mouth hung open as Jeb gently touched her wrist. She didn't pull away.

"I shouldn't have gone along with it—the not telling you part—and I know it was wrong. But I didn't know how else to talk with you, to get to know you. The last few months have been the best in my life, and I didn't want that to stop. For me, it has been like I was always waiting on you to get here. To Rocky Ridge and me." He laughed lowly and then his chuckle faded as the train came into the station.

Rowena kept staring at Jeb, her brow furrowed. With her heart pounding in her chest, she gripped her bag tightly against her as a defense. The man had been in the heat too long and was mixing up his words. "I think you should sit down," she managed. "You must be tired." And she looked down as he gently grasped one of her hands and pulled it towards him.

"I care for you more than I have cared for anyone else," Jeb told her. "Please, let me make this up to you. You are a beautiful woman, Rowena, and I admire your strength and your character. And, the truth is that you deserve better than to be kept in the dark about important matters. So let me fix this, please. I love you, and I want you to stay. With me."

She felt the air leave her lungs as she gaped at him. Exhaling sharply, she stepped back and bumped into the wall again. A lump formed in her throat and she eyed him suspiciously as he stepped closer. "You w-what? I don't understand... I..."

"All aboard!" Rowena jumped at the exclamation from the platform. She looked through wide eyes as the other people around them began to board the train. She recalled the handwritten free pass in her pocket that would allow her to get to Denver. But her legs felt sluggish and she couldn't move. She also recalled that she had no money. But the most important detail she recalled was Jeb's admission. He loved her. She shook her head and tried to straighten out her thoughts.

"Please. Stay a little longer, at the very least. Give me a chance to right this wrong. I'd like another chance. Please?"

"My train..." she leaned in that direction, but still couldn't move. Groaning in frustration, Rowena shook her head. All she wanted to do was yell and scream at him, wondering why he was trying to confuse her. But as she opened her mouth, she realized what he was really saying.

The man was proposing to her.

"What?" She blinked. "Wait, I…you…"

"I love you," Jeb told her firmly. "Please, let me show you that I'm sincere. I know you don't trust me because of the matchmaking with Susannah. But I want you to see that my motive was never to deceive you. I only wanted to get to know you."

She looked away, but didn't take a step to board the train.

"If you decide you can't forgive me after I've tried to make it up to you, then I'll buy your train ticket. Wherever you like, no matter what. But I want to prove to you, Rowena, that I'm better than this. And I want to be better than this, for you."

There was something in his gaze that made her forget about the train. She didn't hear the last call, nor the whistle that blew as the machine started off again. But she realized in this moment that she had her freedom. He was asking, not telling her to stay. It was her decision to make.

All Rowena knew was the look in his eyes, something she had only ever seen once before. It was in the gaze that Lucas had had for Susannah, and something in her heart said that it was good. So Rowena used the freedom she worked so hard to hold on to.

"All right," she said finally. "I'll stay."

Chapter Nineteen

"I think it would be more along the lines of luck," Lucas's low voice could be heard in the hallway. "If anything." They could see his shadow through the crack of the doorway. Rowena heard Susannah chuckle behind her.

"I don't know." Susannah sighed deeply. "It turned out all right now, didn't it?"

Rowena rolled her eyes with a snort. Twisting her hands together in her lap, she turned to the mirror, hardly recognizing the young girl staring back at her. If anything, she didn't look like a girl any longer, but a woman.

"By luck or the grace of God," Lucas reminded her, drumming his fingers against the wall. "And that's why we're changing that advert. You're going to be completely clear about this. I think Rowena here will be more than eager to keep you in check."

The woman just huffed but when she caught Rowena's gaze in the mirror, she offered a sheepish smile.

"I know he's right, but he doesn't have to be so happy about it," she whispered with a wink.

"I heard that," Lucas snorted.

Rowena just rolled her eyes, knowing she shouldn't get involved when the Jessups were teasing each other. Instead, she glanced at the mirror again. In such a short amount of time, it seemed so impossible for everything to have changed. "Thank you." She nodded to Susannah when the woman pinned the final curl.

Mrs. Jessup beamed. "You're a lovely bride, Rowena. Jeb won't know what to say. I can't wait to see the look on his face. Now, are you ready?"

"I can't wait to see Jeb, either. I just hope he didn't cut his face shaving this morning." Rowena laughed and looked at herself in the mirror again. "Yes, I'm ready."

"Horses are ready, too," Lucas called from the other side, his hearing practically perfect. "And they're probably cold. And I have your cloaks right here."

Humming, Susannah obeyed and opened the door to her husband. They talked quietly as Rowena studied herself one last time. Dark curls framed her oval face, with that pointy chin of hers. She didn't like it, but Jeb did. He seemed to like just about everything if it involved her. And at the thought of the man, she couldn't help but smile.

It had been a long journey, she acknowledged. The Jessups had apologized, and set her up in the town's hotel for a few days until Rowena recovered from her hurt. After enough talking and clearing the air, she had grudgingly returned to their home. Repairing the relationship had been difficult but with Jeb's convincing,

Rowena had worked on it and the two women had developed a steady friendship as a result.

That was when she wasn't spending her time with Jeb, of course. She hadn't known what she was getting into after accepting his idea to stay longer, but today she wouldn't want to be anywhere else. The man had settled her doubts, erased her fears, and today she felt like a whole new woman.

Standing up, she went to meet the Jessups in the front of the house. Rowena walked carefully as she glanced around there, realizing that this was no longer her home. For the better part of the year it was everything she had known. There was so much that had happened, good and bad, so many lessons that she had needed to learn.

It made her think of that night. "I would never hurt you." Jeb had offered that grin of his, putting out a hand. "Come on, or you'll miss the best part." It was in the middle of a rain storm, and he had come out riding to meet her for their usual Tuesday supper. It had rained all day, so Rowena was certain he wouldn't come. Yet he had, and then he had dragged her out into the rain.

She had scoffed. "You might not, but the weather says otherwise." Crossing her arms, she wrinkled her nose. Already the dampness was affecting her hair and she fixed her braid. "It's not safe out there."

Jeb's frown caught her off guard just then because so little bothered him. "But…" he trailed off with a furrowed brow. "Rowena, I really do want you to see this. I swear, I'm not putting you in danger. I want to share something that I've been wanting to show you for a while. You'll be safe with me."

She had gathered her courage and reluctantly stepped

forward, knowing what she had to do. Lightning struck again behind her and she whipped around, but by then it was already gone. So she took a deep breath, and touched his arm.

"Do you promise me that we'll be safe?" She meant for the words to come out stronger, but they came out as a soft whisper.

"Of course," he told her. "I would never let anything bad happen to you." Those words were so simple to him. Even after she had told him all about her struggles growing up, the man hadn't changed the way he saw her or treated her. Jeb brought his horse around, and she climbed up in front of him as they started out into the storm.

The rain poured and even with his hat she didn't know how the man could see anything. But she trusted him as he asked, and allowed him to take her to the place he had in mind. They stopped in a field where he jumped down and held his arms out to help her down.

She stumbled into his arms from the horse, and realized he was laughing as he took off his hat. Shaking his head, he took her hand and turned her around where he pointed to the tall peaks ahead where the storm raged on.

At the first strike, Rowena jumped for she was certain they were too close. But Jeb's hand tightened around hers, and her heart pattered. By the third strike, Rowena started to realize why they were there. The brightness of the lightning lit up the valleys below and the mountains above, creating a wondrous view. Relaxing, she leaned against Jeb and he wrapped an arm around her. They were soaked, but it didn't matter.

It was then that Rowena realized this overwhelming and exhausting feeling in her heart was something more. He had wanted so badly to show her this view. It made her grin as she thought about his childish antics. But they were fun to indulge, and he was good company. Rowena had thought that she needed to be alone to have her independence, but she was learning that was not the case. Turning to the man who had dragged her out into the middle of a storm with a promise only their God could keep, Rowena had wrapped her arms around him and leaned up to kiss him.

"Do you hate the view that much?" he chuckled against her lips.

His breath was warm against her cheek as she hugged him tightly, trying not to shiver. "It's spectacular. I understand what you mean now," she added, speaking of several things in one. And she kissed him again, to make sure he understood.

As they pulled away reluctantly, knowing how improper this was, Jeb's grin broadened. "Good," he said finally. "I couldn't be happier."

And they stayed there watching the storm until she began to shiver. Once they returned to the house, he stayed late so the two of them wrapped themselves tightly into blankets around the Jessup fireplace to talk quietly and share a piece of sweet potato pie. By morning, they had a wedding date.

"Whoa, Lucas!" Susannah laughed as they hit a hole in the road and Rowena jerked back from her sweet memories. Clutching her cloak tightly, she pulled up the hood and looked around. They were nearly to town. In fact, if she turned to her left…yes, there was his house. Their house, she corrected herself.

It had three rooms now, a cozy little place that she was ready to share with Jeb. If she looked hard enough, she could see the three flower pots beside the front door with small sunflowers struggling to grow.

"Here we are!" Lucas called as the chapel came into sight. She turned, her heart hammering as they arrived and headed inside. Her fingers fumbled for the clasp of her cloak and her gaze fell upon Jeb.

Their eyes met, and instantly they grinned. Before she knew it, Susannah had put the bouquet in her hands and she was facing Jeb Harbin as Pastor Simmons talked. He was a lovely speaker, but it was hard to focus on anything but the tall man before her with that dashing and devilish grin.

"Hello," he whispered to her.

"Hello," she whispered back.

"Are you ready?"

"Yes. Are you ready?"

"More than ready."

"Good."

"Very good."

It was a blur all until the pastor proclaimed the close. "Before God and these witnesses, I now pronounce you husband and wife."

Rowena looked up to Jeb who took a step closer, though not quite closing the gap. It was just enough of an invitation. And he waited with a big grin and those bright eyes. She was free to do whatever she wished. And she knew exactly what she wanted to do with that freedom. Rowena stepped forward and only then did

Jeb wrap his arms around her, and their lips met for their first kiss as a married couple.

Every kiss was a promise that banished her fears. It was as though the past had never happened, for the pain and doubt left when Jeb was there. He cared for her in a way that she had never known was possible.

She thanked God quickly for Susannah and Lucas. Without them, she'd never have met Jeb. Then she thanked God for Jeb who had shown her in so many ways what love really meant.

* * * * *

OLIVIA AND SIMON

Chapter One

Rocky Ridge, Colorado; 1881

Bedsheets, check. Curtains, check. Pillows, check. Fresh pot of flowers by the window, check. Susannah Jessup rocked back and forth on her feet, reviewing the room one last time. One last time for the day, anyway.

With a critical gaze, she surveyed the set up and tried to imagine coming here for the first time, and that she had never set foot here before. Would she be comfortable, feel safe? Finally satisfied there was nothing else she could do, Susannah closed the door behind her and checked on the next room.

The boarding house had six rooms, meaning that six young women were able to reside there, to live and adjust and create a life. There were four on the ground floor, with two in the attic. After glancing in the last room, Susannah stared at the hall, pausing reflectively.

"It's going to work," she whispered to herself firmly. But this wasn't a concern of hers. She believed with all her heart that soon this house would be bustling and full of life, of people learning and growing. It wasn't quite the same thing as children, she acknowledged, but it would still be lovely. And she was happy.

Lost in her thoughts, Susannah went to her new office where she found her files, wanting to make sure she hadn't forgotten a thing. Shuffling through them, the folders were resorted once again as she changed her mind on who to focus on next. After Jeb Harbin, it was hard to decide which man to start with, especially since she didn't have any other women there yet.

The new file on top was Simon James. It was one of the newest ones, for he was a friend of Jeb's and she had practically promised him everything before finishing his portfolio. A good young man, he used to work on the railways before coming out west to start over again. Though he lived with his sister and her family, he was clearly working hard to make his own way. Jeb had mentioned the man to her several times before Mr. James ever stepped over her threshold.

Hopefully, Susannah prayed, there would be someone there for him soon. The man had been through his share of troubles, and she wanted him to find something good in life. And finding love would be a very good thing.

What could be better than love? To find someone to cherish through the sunlight and the dark nights, someone to laugh with and cry with, someone to build a fuller life with. The world was complicated enough and if she could help, Susannah would do whatever she could to bring people together. Now that she had Simon James on the string, she just needed to find someone right for him.

With the evening progressing, she returned to the kitchen to finish up the supper she had left on the stove. Humming, she brought out the hot cast iron pot and turned, setting it on the table just as her husband, Lucas, walked in.

It was nearly impossible to hear him until he showed up in the room, but she was slowly getting better at not jumping. Heart hammering, she took a deep breath and tossed the nerves aside. Giving him a look, she set the food down and closed the stove. "There you are. You're a little late, aren't you?" She paused, noticing he was limping. Hastening to his side as he sat, Susannah frowned. "Whatever happened?"

She pulled out her towel at the sight of blood. Below his knee, the pant leg was soaked in it. The only reason she didn't scream was because she was used to his occasional injuries, and he didn't look to be in too much pain.

"It was just a horse," he informed her hurriedly. More than anything, he sounded irritated as he shifted in his seat and sighed. "He was nervous, and the bridle was too tight. I fixed it."

She gave him a look. "But you didn't fix yourself."

"I did," he frowned, and pulled up his pant leg for her to find a bandage, already blood-soaked but he raised an eyebrow not understanding how his effort fell short. "See?" He was dangerous enough for people, but apparently he was also dangerous to himself. His days of being a Texas Ranger had taught him to bind injured body parts, but there was little finesse to it. "See? Nothing to worry about." But he stopped as she went to a corner cabinet, pulling out fresh bandages.

"You and your horses," she murmured, returning to his side. "You and your trouble. Was there no one to help you?"

Lucas watched as she started pulling the bandages away. "Yes, half the town. But nobody goes after a horse racing down the streets. It was Farmer Calloway's new stallion, just arrived from Texas, apparently. He spent a fortune but didn't know how to treat him."

Sighing, Susannah dumped the bloody bandages in a bowl and started running them under the sink. The fresh cut was nasty but it was hardly bleeding and that was a good sign. She tended to it and cleaned it as he told her the story.

"Oh, and we had mail," he finished it off with a flourish, pulling out two bent letters from his pockets.

For a minute he toyed with them, preventing her from grabbing them. She reached out, but Lucas danced them around her. Susannah laughed, shaking her head at him before lightly punching the knee on his unhurt leg. It would have no effect on a man of his stature, but he played off a wince and handed over the papers.

Climbing up to her feet, she put the towel down and wiping her forehead, glanced them over curiously. There was something about mail, about having it arrive and wondering who it could be from and what it said.

One was from her aunt in Boston, and Susannah beamed. She was about to open that one first until the other caught her eye. She didn't recognize the handwriting and it was addressed to the Jessup Boarding House for Women. Gasping in delight, she took a seat and let Lucas off to go change his pants as she opened the letter from a young woman in Vermont.

To the Jessups of the Boarding House in Rocky Ridge, Colorado:

Greetings and I pray all is well. I am a woman from Vermont in need of a place to stay out in the western territories. I am hoping there is space available in your boarding house. Unfortunately, I've already begun my journey and will follow my letter soon after.

There is reason for me to leave town suddenly and I am booked to leave on the first train. If there is not space available when I arrive, that is understandable.

Here are the details about me in case I will be welcomed. My name is Olivia Foster, and I have lived in Vermont all my life. My parents grew sick soon after I was born, and I was raised by my grandmother. She taught me everything she knew, and I am skilled in a few basics such as sewing, weaving, and cooking. For the last five years, I've worked under the employment of the town's doctor as a nurse. Soon after my grandmother died, I became betrothed to a good man, but he suffered a terrible accident. Now I fear I have become a burden to his family. I feel a need to be where I am wanted, or at least needed. I believe that your advert offers such, in so many words.

I have a little to pay my way, and I can work hard to earn the rest as I go along. I only pray that my good friend is able to send this off in time and that the post runs quickly. My hope is that I don't arrive before my letter.

May God bless you.
Olivia Foster

Susannah had read it three times before Lucas returned, his hair wet from a quick wash and wearing clean pants that didn't have a spot of blood on them. Her heart pattered as she looked up, having mixed feelings about the contents of the letter. The moment she caught her husband's gaze, though, she forgot everything in his smile.

Strolling over, Lucas took the seat beside her. "Hello."

"Hello." Susannah let him kiss her cheek before the plates were put in front of them.

"Who was the letter from?"

She waited until he said Grace to answer his question. "A young lady. Miss Olivia Foster," Susannah announced. He looked up at her, fork in hand, and waited for her to continue. His gaze was unreadable. "She is already on her way here. She sounds skilled, and is in desperate need of a new home."

"Then it's good a thing we have one here for her," he commented lightly, filling her mug with hot tea.

She set a large piece of cornbread on his plate and pushed the pot of butter towards him. "Indeed it is," Susannah nodded, smiling. She stood up to go to him and leaned down to kiss him when she was close enough. He hadn't shaved that morning, so his scruff was coming in quite nicely and was prickly against her cheek. Rubbing a hand over it lightly, she shook her head at him. "I thought you were going to stay clean shaven this summer?"

Kissing her hand, Lucas leaned back. "We'll see. I thought you liked the beard?"

Winking at him, she picked up her fork. "We'll see. Now, about Miss Foster. I was thinking she could take a room on the ground floor? And perhaps I'll make some muffins in preparation of her arrival. Trains move so quickly now, so I think she'll be here before the week is out."

Chapter Two

The memory was vague. Hazy. A kind face, framed with soft curls and the sweetest smile. There were wrinkles in her face and the curls were white, but she could clearly see the love in those eyes. Clinging to the memory, Olivia Foster remembered her grandmother's sweet face and pondered what the woman would think of her now.

A tear escaped, and she hurriedly wiped it away. Sniffling, she closed her family's Bible, after stopping to read her favorite passage. The book went into the bag, along with her other shawl. By then, her valise was full and she clasped it shut. Buttoning the cloak she wore, the young lady marched over to the door and gave one final sweeping gaze around the place she had so recently called home.

Even then Olivia could recall the first day she had arrived, light with hope and joy. It was a sweet home filled with good people at the time, people who she had thought cared about her. Strange how time changed things. Swallowing hard, she closed the door quietly and walked down the hall until she was outside. Winter was ending, but these mountains had hardly noticed. A chill entered her bones and she shivered, but kept moving. She couldn't stop now.

The sun was getting ready to rise, and she was late.

Wrapping her arms close around herself and clutching the bag tightly, she made her way down the street and over several blocks. Her eyes darted around everywhere, soaking it all in for the last time. Walking quickly, soon she was out of breath and panting before she made it to the stage coach. Too north for anyone to care, Vermont lacked trains and she would need to catch a ride to New York to reach one.

"Hold up!" She called, seeing the horses geared up and ready to go. Waving an arm, she shouted in the streets, her heart leaping out of her throat. "Please!" They stopped and the driver glanced back. "I'm coming!" Her breath came out in white puffs as she hastened to reach the wagon.

"You're holding us up," the man said gruffly, eyeing her critically. He glanced at the road and then sighed, hopping down. "Come along, now. It's a nickel through each station. Have you any bags? We have a schedule to be on."

She shook her head, and handed over a quarter. "I'm going to New York. This is all I have. You can take me there, right? Where I can find a train?" Though she tried to smile politely, she was too out of breath.

He stroked his beard and then shrugged before climbing back up into his seat. "Most likely. Get in, then." There were only three other people inside, but they opened the door and she clambered in. It was stuffy and bumpy but it would get her to safety.

Olivia looked around, still gasping for breath as she glanced at the people and then outside where the town was rolling by. It was the entire life she had known, rolling away and soon to be gone forever. She could hardly imagine such a thing. These folks must have come from the border themselves and were headed down to the larger cities to find work. At least that's what she'd heard they did when they came to America. But there were so few that left her small Vermont town.

She gulped and settled back in her seat. She was doing this for a new life. For a safe future, she told herself. She wanted to, and she had to. Trying to ignore the lump forming in her throat, Olivia sorted through her plan again. It wasn't much of one, but it was still better than what had been in store for her.

There was a lot of time to think over the next few days as she made her transition from stagecoach to train, and it was still another five days to reach Colorado. Olivia Foster reflected on all those that she was leaving behind, everyone resting in Elder Grove. Her family, her fiancé, she was leaving them all behind.

"Forgive me," she mouthed quietly, and leaned back in her seat on the train. Tightening her grip on her valise, Olivia shifted and then stared at her hands. They were scratched and pricked, but white and clean. She was good at that much. Rubbing the dry and flaking skin away, she sighed.

If anything, she would also miss Dr. Hadley and his practice. The man had taken her in five years ago to act as a nurse in the office, teaching her valuable skills and bringing in a small income for her and her frail grandmother. Dr. Hadley was a good man who was growing in his years with a healthy sense of humor and generous nature. He had been kind to drop the letter off for her yesterday afternoon, before she had returned home to pack.

He had listened carefully as she had explained her plan. It was risky and may not work, but it was better than nothing and better than what was in store for her there. "But they can't force you to marry someone." Dr. Hadley had looked at her with a creased brow. "Surely they want what is best for you, my dear?"

With a strained smile, she had handed him her letter with a nickel. "I'm afraid it's not as simple as that. We're not family, we never had the chance to…" Olivia had swallowed hard and tried not to say anything mean. They were a good family, just misled. She was certain of it. When Jack had been around, nothing like this would have happened.

Her friend wouldn't understand what this meant, for he was just another man who could control his destiny. Men had it more easily in their world, and she accepted this. But they wouldn't control hers, unless she had exhausted every effort first. Of course the Hendersons were a nice family and they had offered her a place to live when her grandmother had died. Had Jack survived, they would have been married and there would be no trouble at all.

But Jack had died in the accident, and the Hendersons thought differently now. She couldn't blame them, but it meant she had to change things before they made plans that she didn't want to be a part of.

"Can you please send this off before you reach home?" she had asked him again. "And I'm sorry for providing such short notice. But I do believe Mrs. Rachel Hyland will be most helpful in replacing me here. She's a wonderful midwife and could use the extra income."

Sighing, Dr. Hadley had gone through his drawers, and pulled out his wallet. "Then the least I can do is ensure your safe arrival. Here is your pay, along with a bonus. You have done more than enough work here, and as good as Mrs. Hyland is, I don't think she's nearly as tidy as you are. I hope you taught her your tricks."

Olivia blushed, and grudgingly accepted the bills. She swallowed hard. Frowning, she shook her head. "Oh, sir, that's too much. Please, I'll just fine."

He patted her shoulder and smiled through his thick mustache. "You may need it, Olivia. You've been so good, I don't want anything to happen to you, dear. You deserve better than this, after everything you've been through. You'll be safe, won't you?"

Swallowing hard, she had nodded several times. "Yes, yes of course. Thank you so much, Dr. Hadley. You've been so good to me, truly. Thank you!" She hugged him one last time, and left through the door.

It broke her heart. Leaving the only life she had ever known, she wondered if it was the right choice. But to count everything she had and everything she had lost, it was clear that she had little else to keep her in Vermont. The familiarity was all she had, but little comfort. Besides, if she stayed, there was little of that familiar life that she would be able to keep if things went the way that the Hendersons had decided upon.

Now, on the train, Olivia sighed and patted her pockets carefully. The money was still there. Taking a deep breath, she glanced outside just as the train conductor announced the next stop. Her stop. At last, Rocky Ridge, Colorado was waiting for her.

Chapter Three

He hadn't felt this anxious in a long time. Glancing down at his sweaty palms, the man hurriedly wiped them on the side of his trousers so it wouldn't show. Simon James glanced around again, resting a hand on the back of his horse.

It was a lovely place, a large farmhouse with a stable and a barn nearby. He could see the pasture stretching lazily out behind the barn with a fence built to keep the horses inside. And right behind the pastures were the purple mountains reaching for the sky. It was probably the best view in all of Colorado.

He knew it was, but the joy he normally felt at something so perfect simply wasn't there. His stomach was in knots and he was too nervous to truly enjoy the view right now. Swallowing, he rubbed his hands together and forced himself to head towards the big house.

It had been months now since he first tried to make it here, but he'd never made it this far. Usually he got to the middle of the road leading in and there he'd turn around and go back home.

But today he wouldn't turn back. He made his way across the yard and up the steps to the porch. There was a bench and two chairs there for people to enjoy the sunset. The windows were open in the room nearby, with curtains trailing out with the breeze. They were white with lace. He smiled at the thought of a home with a woman's touch.

The thought brought her to mind, the petite brunette who continued to haunt his dreams. She always smiled at him, wracking him with guilt. Even now he could hear her laughter in the wind and it made him hesitate, a fist hanging in the air and ready to knock. But he couldn't bring himself to do it. No matter how tightly he squeezed his eyes tightly shut, she wouldn't leave him.

Sighing, Simon finally dropped his fist and turned to leave, only to find Lucas Jessup coming up the road. The man waved his hat before placing it back on his head as he drew closer. Instead of taking his horse to the barn, he drew up close to the porch and swung down, hurrying up to the man. "Good day! Simon, isn't it? Simon James?"

They shook hands and Simon managed a shaky smile. With a nod, he pushed back his dark blond hair. "Yes, um—that's me. Simon."

"Yes." Lucas nodded. "Right. Well, do come on in. I'm sure my Susie is nearly ready for supper and we're always happy for some company." He opened the door and stepped through.

He was caught now. Trapped. Simon swallowed. Slowly he followed Lucas into the house, closing the door behind him as he put his hat down and shed the jacket. The other man led the way through the house, down the hall and towards a delightful smell.

"I hear you this time," a woman sang out. "You're losing your edge, Lucas, I—" she turned with a grin and paused, seeing two men there. "Oh. Company."

She pouted as her husband went over to kiss her cheek. He recognized the woman from town, often seen arm in arm with her husband. She was short with the bluest eyes and the longest blonde hair he'd ever seen. A blush bloomed across her cheeks with her husband's touch.

Simon stood there awkwardly, and dropped his gaze to give them a moment's privacy. He briefly thought that perhaps he could just slip back out the door, but that seemed silly when he thought about it for another second. His courage had failed him, and he shouldn't have allowed the man to invite him in, but what was he supposed to say? Anything but coming in would be very rude.

"I was close," he heard Mrs. Jessup mumble.

"You say that every time," Mr. Jessup responded. "Susannah, my darling, this is Mr. Simon James. He was just headed to our house and I came upon him. Would you mind if he stayed for supper?"

The woman laughed as though it were a joke. She set down the big cast iron pot and wiped her hands on her apron. "As if you need to ask me such a thing. There's always enough food to go around. Good evening, Mr. James. It's a pleasure to meet you. You're most welcome at our table tonight, that is if you like venison."

"Well, um, ma'am," he stammered. "It's swell to meet you, too. And, I suppose I do, um, like venison."

Mrs. Jessup grinned and gestured to the table. "Splendid! Please take a seat, then. My husband will set another place. And of course you like potatoes?"

He nodded. Before he could speak again, she kept on going.

"Perfect, perfect. Yes, here's a spot for you right across from me. Now, where do you hail from, sir? I don't believe I quite recognize you."

"You probably wouldn't," he managed bashfully as he took the assigned seat. Simon hesitated as he watched the other man bring him a plate and mug, and then leaving again to get him utensils. Clearing his throat uncomfortably, he shifted in his seat. "I've only come to these hereabouts a few months ago. I've been staying with my sister. Her name is Lillian James—well, Lillian. Dane now. She married Frank Dane a while ago. He has a ranch nearby."

Her eyes lit up. "Lillian! Of course I know her. She has the cutest children. Loud, but cute. And she always brings the best berry pies to the dances. Yes, I see it now. You two have the same smile."

Simon managed an uneasy smile as they started into polite conversation, but he could only provide a few short and vague answers. All the same, the Jessups were welcoming and kind, doing their best to make him feel right at home. It wasn't a feeling he had experienced in a long time.

His turbulent belly had just started to settle down when they were finishing the stew. Mrs. Jessup asked the question that would lead into the subject he'd almost decided to ignore and the rumbling in his stomach returned immediately.

"I must say, Mr. James, we've loved having your company this evening. I'm so glad you came by. Lucas said you were already headed towards our home, is that correct? Is there anything we can do to help you? I'd hate for your visit to be incomplete if there's a specific need you were aiming to fulfill."

He had just been wiping his face with his napkin and froze. Slowly he put it down and clenched it in his fists. Both sets of eyes fell on him as he hesitated, taking a deep breath. Should he say it? Or was he done with these attempts? Perhaps it was a sign. But even as the doubts crowded in, Simon James found himself confessing the truth.

"Well, Jeb Harbin and I have been talking, you see. And, um, since you brought him and his wife together," Simon stammered. "He was thinking…well, I suppose I was thinking, about getting married again."

Susannah looked over at Lucas and then back at Simon. Her brow knitted together in confusion. "Again?"

Simon looked down and drew in his breath. Then he looked back at Susannah with as much confidence as he could muster. "Um, yes. You see, my wife died a few years ago. Before I came out here. Her name was Jane, and I…my sister thinks it's time I moved on, and I guess she's right. I'd like to try. Jeb said you ran a boarding house for women getting married, or wanting to. So I thought I would try to stop by and talk to you about it. I should have told you this right from the start."

Mrs. Jessup waved a hand in the air. "Nonsense! You told me as you felt you could. But if you'd told me when you arrived, we could have had dessert first."

Her smile was contagious and Simon blinked back at her then grinned.

She stood and then paused as her face turned sympathetic. "Mr. James, I'm terribly sorry about your wife. That must have been a terrible time in your life." Susannah looked over at Lucas and the two of them shared a look. "It's a remarkable thing you're doing to get back into life again. We'd love to help. How about you two get dessert ready, and I'll pull out the applications."

"Applications?" Simon's eyes widened in surprise.

But she'd already left the room. Lucas chuckled and clapped the man on his shoulder. "Don't worry," he assured the younger man. "It'll be all right. It's a painless process. Well, mostly."

Chapter Four

"Let's begin, shall we?"

Susannah fixed her skirt, settling into her chair and then looked over at Mr. Simon James on the other side of the table. She beamed and tried to pull back the grin since she could see that he was nervous.

The man shifted uncomfortably, testing out the arm-rests and leaning back only to lean forward again. Then he tugged at his jacket and offered her a tight smile. "I suppose we might."

Chuckling, she shook her head. "Please, relax. There's no need to worry over this. This is just an opportunity for me to learn about you, and who you are. By knowing you, I can find the sort of woman you're looking for, as well as one who fits you. And if we're lucky, someone who has been looking for your type as well. Do you understand?"

He cleared his throat twice before nodding, keeping his gaze down at his hands clenched in his lap. The man had high cheekbones that looked sharper now that he'd combed his hair back. Susannah cocked her head as she studied him, for just an instant he'd looked just a little like her Lucas. The cheekbones had done it. But their jawlines were distinctly different, she noted, and her husband's hair and eyes were darker.

Had he been that nervous when they first met? For a minute her mind went back into her memories as she tried to recall that time so many years ago. It had been cold, and she'd felt so lost. Lucas Jessup had ridden up and saved her, giving her a life she never would have dreamed of before. Somehow he'd always managed to look so confident, with that highbrow and sharp gaze. Then Susannah blinked, and saw Simon James again.

"Wonderful." She smiled and opened her folder. Picking up her pen, she asked him, "So, tell me about yourself. I'll write down anything I think might be relevant. Where did you grow up?"

Nodding, he locked his jaw twice before saying anything. "I grew up just outside Boston. A small town without a name. We had a small farm, but it never did very well. My mother maintained it while my father worked the rails. When we were old enough to walk, my sister and I started to help.

"She worked in the yard and I carried my father's toolbox. Then when I was fourteen, I signed on and worked my own labors on the rails. It kept us from starving through the winter, since our farm produced so little. I remember one year we tried to grow pumpkins, since it would bring us something better in the market, but the entire patch was eaten by bugs."

Susannah nodded soberly. "It sounds like it was a difficult time."

His was a grim smile. "It was." For a minute he was

quiet, and she could see something was weighing on him. Simon's eyes were closed and she watched him thoughtfully, not saying a thing. Just when Susannah was about to offer the opportunity to finish this another time, he sighed heavily and straightened up in his seat. "I knew Jane for most of my life, and three years ago I married her."

That was unexpécted. Susannah wrote that down immediately, scrawling carefully though he stopped again. She finished writing and the room fell quiet. Hesitantly she glanced up at him, trying to read his troubled gaze. "You don't need to continue if—"

"She died in an accident only a few months after we married." The words tumbled out quickly off his tongue, and it took her a moment to decipher them. "It's been more than two years. Now I've come out here to start fresh and help out my sister and her husband. Our parents died, and I sold the farm. I do the train management for this area in Colorado now."

Susannah didn't know how to write this down. She hadn't had to deal with a case like this yet, and knew it would be a prelude to the others for previously married folks in her matchmaking business. Biting her tongue, she carefully wrote down a note or two and then turned to him with a gentle smile.

"That must have been very difficult, to endure it even now and in speaking with me. Thank you for trusting me with the truth, Mr. James. Now, how would you describe your daily routine? Is it the same every day?"

His gaze brightened. "A little, yes. I sleep in the barn, in a room we built in the loft. I like having my own area. Frank, my brother-in-law, tends to the ranch and I help him out as I get the day started. Lately I tend to the cows, but the children are often nearby, playing with the chickens or the goats. I usually get a little distracted and spend a minute or two with them and their games. Then there's family time over breakfast." He smiled, seeming to think kindly of his sister's children.

"That sounds like a lovely way to start the day." Susannah nodded at his obvious love of his family.

He gave her a quick nod. "Sometimes, I take the children to the school house or help on the ranch. That's only if I'm not working at the railroad, of course. The channels for the train out west weren't as firmly built as in the east, you see. They only had half the crew and were in too big of a rush to get it all in place. I replace the iron bars and of course, there's the occasional problem with the broad gauges. If it's far away, I camp out there for the night but most of my work can be done within the day."

"It sounds like an important job, Simon." Susannah raised an eyebrow as she nodded.

He shrugged. "Maybe. And then if I return in time, there's supper and an evening reading of the Holy Bible. I, um, I don't go into town too often. Only for church and groceries when my sister doesn't have the time."

Susannah wrote hurriedly, scrambling to catch all the necessary words to keep in his portfolio. "Good, good, thank you. It sounds like a busy life, and a good one. And now, Mr. James, what are you looking for in the days to come, in your future?"

He was quiet for a good long while, and she began wondering if he hadn't heard her. She peeked over her folder and opened her mouth to repeat the question, but she stopped. Susannah bit her lip as something told her to wait.

"That's a good question," he murmured roughly. "I hadn't considered too much of it lately, only that I... well, a woman in my life," he started with a shy smile. "A home. I'm considering making a stake, or um, building a spot in town. Eventually I'd like to have a family. Yes, a family would be mighty nice." He trailed off, nodding absently.

Cocking her head, the young woman studied him thoughtfully. "It would be nice, indeed. Thank you for your time, Mr. James. That's all I have for today. Now, I usually ask for at least three references, and I can either meet with them or they can bring me letters. And after perhaps another conversation, over dinner, I'm sure, we can see where we are. Does that sound acceptable?"

Hastily he stood, fiddling with the fraying hem of his shirt. "Yes, of course. That sounds good. Right, I'll get you some references, then. I'll talk to them tomorrow, if that's all right with you?"

Susannah beamed, and led him out. Mr. James left as quietly as he had come, and she watched him from her porch as he rode off. She was preparing to step inside just as she found dust kicking up from the other direction, from the direction of town. Her heart skipped a beat as she hoped Lucas was coming home sooner than expected.

Chapter Five

The further she drove from Vermont, the more Olivia grew anxious about her decision. She had trouble sitting still, she couldn't concentrate on reading, and she had difficulty sleeping.

Doubts crept into her mind like shadows in the corners, making her wonder if she was truly alone. That no one was watching her. Surely Jack's family would move on, without her there. Wouldn't they? It's not that the Hendersons were cruel, by any means, but lately... well, things had been uncomfortable. She shuddered and hurried down the steps of the train depot.

Dust gathered around her feet as she looked about her. So, this was Rocky Ridge, Colorado. Scrunching her nose, she tried to decide on her next step as she looked around carefully, watching the sights all around her. Gulping, she took it all in. It was a pretty sight, somewhat similar to her hometown with the colors and patterned streets. The bustling people moving around as though she wasn't there.

It took her a minute to pull herself together and start

walking. She shivered in the chilly wind as she started moving. Clutching her bag close, she made her way up the street and found a general store. It was as good as any place, she decided, and headed right inside. It was a large space, filled with many things that she had not seen before. Many leather items, and what looked like cowhide blankets, items she'd never had in Vermont.

Swallowing, she went up to the register where there was a man sorting candy and glancing around from time to time. He was short with gray hair and a thick mustache that just about matched his hair. Her heart thumped as she reached him, even as he smiled and nodded her way. "Howdy, ma'am. What can we do for you today?"

"I need to get somewhere," she explained articulately. "But I'm not sure where it is. Would you know where to find the Jessup's Boarding House?"

Chuckling, he nodded as he pulled out a piece of candy and popped it in his mouth. It crunched loudly in the quiet shop. "I sure as do. It's about five miles west of here."

Her smile faded. "Oh." That was a long walk, and she was already so tired. Glancing towards the door, Olivia tried to prepare herself for the very long stroll ahead of her. "All right. Well, thank you. West, then."

She was about to turn away when he cleared his throat. She looked back at him with a raised brow and he waved her back to him. "It's a long walk, for sure. If you have time to wait, I'm sure there'll be someone headed out that way soon enough." He cleared his throat again and looked across the room.

Olivia nodded, but had no idea what to say. She considered starting out with the hope that someone would come by as she walked. Before she could make a decision, the man gestured again.

"Well, look at that, would you?" He raised his voice. "Michael! My good man. You're headed home soon, aren't you?"

A man tipped his hat in their direction. "Sure am, Sam. Why you need to know?"

Sam waved him over. "This young lady needs to see the Jessups. Can you take her with you? You brought the wagon, right?"

Michael nodded, glancing at the young woman curiously. She dropped her gaze, spotting the ring on his finger. "I sure did. I think I can manage that. Just give me five minutes, and I'll be right over there." Then he wandered the shelves, looking for whatever it was that he needed. After, he returned with two bolts of thick cloth with some flour and sugar. Heaving everything onto the counter, he nodded to Sam and turned to Olivia. "Hey, there. I'm Michael. You're heading over to the Jessups?"

"Yes." She nodded hesitantly, still clutching her bag close. "That's right. They, um—they're expecting me." Olivia wasn't even sure that was true, but it seemed important to add some surety into the mix. They at least knew of her, or she hoped they did. If her letter had arrived, she wouldn't be telling a fib.

The man grinned widely, accepting her words easily. Either he believed her because he didn't mind, or it was because the Jessups were good people. Her stomach fluttered.

"Sounds good. They love company. Let me get all

this loaded up, and we'll deliver you right over there."
And he was honest, for soon she was settled onto his
cart and headed down the bumpy trail.

As they came over the hill, Michael pointed out the
house. Olivia Foster had never been so glad to see something in her life. The weariness seeping into her bones
made it hard to keep her eyes open, even as it was a
pretty sight. It was a lovely little place nestled against
the mountains, surrounded in swarthy green with a
pretty barn behind the main house. As they moved off
the main road, she found there was already a woman
standing on the porch, truly as though she had been
expected.

The bumpy ride had grated on her nerves, and Michael had to help her down, shaky as she was. Olivia
swallowed hard as he turned her towards the house, and
saw the woman headed towards them. She was short
with long blonde hair that trailed down her back and
blew in the breeze. She was beaming as though they
were old friends, her arms outstretched.

"Michael!" she proclaimed, clasping the man's
hands. "How good is it to see you! Is Eleanor well?
And the girls?"

Chuckling, the man nodded and pulled his hat off.
"It's been a while, hasn't it? All my girls are doing well,
of course. It might be time for another supper, if you
and Lucas are feeling up to it?"

She only grinned brighter. "We always are! Lovely
idea there, just lovely." Then she turned over to Olivia,
looking her over for the first time. Her smile barely
dimmed as she looked at the younger woman curiously.
Then she sighed happily and put out her hands. "And

you must be Olivia, I just know it. Miss Olivia Foster. Yes?"

The only thing that kept her jaw from hitting the floor was the fact that she was much too tired to do anything but offer a wane smile. "So my letter reached you in time. Good, yes. Good afternoon."

"I'm Susannah Jessup," the blonde friendly woman introduced herself. "And it's about time you arrived! Welcome, welcome. My dear, you look exhausted. I'm sure you have had such a long journey, so let's get you inside. Michael, would you like to join us?"

He shook his head. "Thank you but no, I'm sure Eleanor is waiting on me. Besides, we're supposed to have a storm headed our way, and I want to make sure we're all bundled down. Will Lucas return here soon?"

She nodded. "He will, yes. That's good to know, Michael, thank you. We'll see you soon. Give our love to Eleanor and the children."

Tipping his hat, he climbed back into the cart. "Sure will. For now, I'll be off. Stay safe in this weather, ladies." And he was gone.

Before she knew it, Olivia was bustled into the house, parted from her bag, and wrapped in a blanket by the fire sipping cider in a very comfortable chair. Curled up in a rocking chair, the young lady sighed as she watched the embers grow red and the flames licking them all about. It was a lovely sight, and she was more than ready to soak it all in. Every muscle cried out in exhaustion, and nothing felt better than doing absolutely nothing for the first time in a long time.

"You look so comfortable." Mrs. Jessup chuckled as

she came over with her own cup of cider. "Good. Have you been traveling nonstop, then?"

She nodded hesitantly, trying to meet her gaze. It was embarrassing to already be so settled in, as though this were her home. "Yes, I'm afraid so. It took longer than expected."

The woman leaned over and patted her knee sympathetically. "Indeed, it always does." She stood up. "I had best start on supper. Sit yourself there until you're nice and warm, why don't you? Then you're free to join me in the kitchen or go to your room. In the boarding house building, yours will be the first door on the right."

"Thank you," Olivia murmured gratefully and she watched the woman walk away. Leaning back in her seat, she let the warmth melt away her inhibitions, and she dozed for most of the day. After waking for good, she found the Jessups finishing up supper, but they saved a portion for her before sending her back to bed for the evening.

Early spring settled in, and so did Olivia. Susannah had a way of making her feel right at home, a feeling she hadn't experienced in a long time. A daily schedule was instituted where she helped at the barn, practiced her stitching, and then helped in the garden. Soon she was practicing to better her reading as well, and her cooking. And that was all within the first two weeks.

Their only hindrance were the questions. Susannah wanted to know everything about her, and it made Olivia nervous. It wasn't that most of her story was dangerous or terrible, but she didn't like everything about her past. Bringing it up only brought back the doubts and the fears. In fact, it was the reason she was here.

Olivia often had the feeling of being watched, but could never tell if it was a good feeling or bad, only noticeable and worrisome. She didn't want to rope anyone else into her troubles, especially since she prayed nightly that they were over.

"It's good to have family around, when it's manageable," Susannah was saying as they worked on the laundry one day. "You were raised by your grandmother then, weren't you? What was she like?"

She took a deep breath. "She was a wonderful woman. Quiet and kind, and she taught me how to knit. After my parents died, Grandmother did everything for me." She paused, sighing with her hands soaking in the chilly water. "She would take me to church, you know, when she could manage it. But I'm afraid her body left her health failing for the large part of our time together. She died a few years ago."

Susannah nodded with a sympathetic smile. "It's never easy losing family. I recently lost a close aunt of mine. We only saw each other a few times during my life back east, but we have written often over the years and I always felt as though she were very close to me. I'm sorry for your loss."

"Thank you," Olivia nodded, brushing her strawberry blonde hair out of her face.

"What happened after that?" Susannah cocked her head. "You had a fiancé, didn't you?"

Swallowing hard, she nodded again. "Yes, I…his family gave me a room in their home, to board until we married." She cleared her throat. "But I'm afraid things didn't go as we had planned. There was an accident. I'm here now, and I'm praying God will guide me in this new direction. When I saw your ad, it just felt right to come here."

She changed the direction of their conversation, hoping that Susannah hadn't noticed. The woman paused thoughtfully, twisting water out a handkerchief. Olivia looked down, taking a deep breath as she did so, praying the woman wouldn't draw them back to the topic of her past again.

She didn't see Susannah hesitate, wiggling her nose before putting on a smile again. "I know exactly what that's like." The married woman looked up and beamed. "And I am certain that He is."

Chapter Six

"Supper?" Simon stammered, fiddling with his hat. "Again?"

Lucas Jessup grinned, crossing his arms. "You can't be tired of my wife's cooking already, can you? Even I'm not and I get that benefit every day."

The man had around ten years on him, and twice the experience in life, in work, and with women. Simon could feel his face growing hot. "No, that's not it, Luc—"

Chuckling, Lucas shook his head and butted in. "It's only a joke. And yes, again. We enjoy your company. Besides, it'll be an evening for friends. We'll have others over as well. We thought we would have you over, along with the Harbins."

Church had come to an end and everyone was milling around the outside of the building to talk that Sunday before heading back home. They glanced around, and they found Jeb and Rowena Harbin talking to the pastor.

The man had been the first person to greet Simon

upon his arrival, before he even found his sister in town. Jeb had brought him to church and to his house to meet Rowena. He'd been a friend to him. They talked little about serious things, but enjoyed jokes and often Jeb joined him on his excursions out to the tracks.

It took him a minute, but then Simon nodded. Lucas would know Jeb because Jeb was Lucas's deputy. Somehow he hadn't made the connection before, but the Jessups would know the Harbins. And the children knew him as well, when they were in town. All the kids in town knew Jeb Harbin. "Yes," he said at last. "Of course."

He was clapped on the back. "Perfect. Tomorrow, at five o'clock. Come hungry," he added, and the man walked away. Simon's gaze traveled after Lucas Jessup, but the man wasn't going back into the crowd to his family. Instead, he waved to the Harbins and turned back into the street, towards his office. It was just at the end of the lane, and Simon watched him disappear.

"Simon, there you are," Lillian touched his arm. "I've been calling for you. The children are ready to go. Are you?"

Blinking, he ruffled his hair and then put his hat back on. It was beginning to rain again and he adjusted his coat so the collar was turned up. Pulling on a smile for his sister, he nodded and glanced around. There he found her two kids arguing over a wooden toy. "Let's be going then, shall we?" He wrapped an arm around his little sister and took the family back to the ranch.

They went inside, where Lillian started on a roast for supper and the children pulled out their hoops and sticks in the yard. Once they were settled, Simon needed his own distraction and went to find Frank out in the field with the cows. They worked together and it kept him focused on each task, fixing the fences and tending to the animals. It wasn't until he was settled in his bed for the evening, exhausted to the bone, that he found himself thinking about the next day's supper.

After all, he'd been through the entire process by then, and Mrs. Jessup had told him that his file was complete and she would keep an eye out for him. Since Lucas had mentioned there would be other guests, that meant it wouldn't be on business. That's when the thought came to him and he inhaled sharply. Did that mean she had found someone?

A knot formed in his throat, and Simon closed his eyes as he felt as though Jane were right there beside him. Her soft touch, her cool hands, her lips whispering in his ear. When he looked around, he found himself alone and started praying though he didn't know why. Simon tossed and turned for most of the night, and woke up with every part of his body and soul aching.

The dread clung to him like a dark cloud as he went through his daily routine that Monday. First the barn animals, and then breakfast. He had to talk with the train station in town, so he took one of the horses and oiled a few spots on the tracks before heading home to clean up. It took him forever to try and get the rank oil off his hands and out of his clothes. But at last, he was dressed and started out of the house.

"Where are you off to?" Lillian noticed him on his way to the door.

Hesitating, Simon swallowed. "Oh, just over to the

Jessups' place. They invited me to supper again. Didn't I tell you?" He tried to smile.

She raised her eyebrow. "You've been there quite a few times. Are you certain they aren't done with their process or program, or whatever it is they call it? Or rather—" she inhaled "—you've completed it and they found you someone?" Lillian brightened as he shifted uncomfortably, still wondering the same thing. "Oh, I bet it is. Do you think it's a girl from town? What about Amy? She's awfully sweet, you know. I always told you—"

"I'm going to be late," he said hurriedly, and went out the door. Taking the horse, he made his way down the lane and to the Jessups' house. His thoughts wandered as they went down the lane, and Simon wondered if he was doing the right thing. By the time he arrived, he still wasn't sure.

"There you are!" Mrs. Jessup beamed as Simon walked through the door. "Come in, come in. Everyone else is already here. No, it's all right. You're just in time." She helped him with his jacket and hat, and guided him to the kitchen. "Let's see, the Harbins are already here. You know them, along with Lucas, of course. Allow me to introduce you to Olivia Foster, a guest of mine. Miss Olivia, this is Simon James. He's recently come west and works with the trains. Now that we're all friends, who's hungry?"

That earned a good chuckle from the party. It put smiles on everyone's faces as they took their seats. Simon was the last one, fiddling uncomfortably with his chair as he swallowed and carefully shot another glance at Olivia. He could tell then that it was as he and his sister had assumed, that Mrs. Jessup had found him a possible match. She was tall, willowy, with reddish-blonde hair and the lightest eyes. It had only made him more nervous, being that close to such a beautiful woman.

She even had lovely poise, and good manners. Simon couldn't focus on anything else, and forgot to eat most of his food. He had no idea how it had even tasted. Most likely it was delightful, as the Jessups always fed him well. Trying to sort through his muddled thoughts was too much work.

Then the young lady laughed at something Jeb said, and he looked up again. "You're too kind." She blushed, and it only made her freckles stand out. "Truly, it's Susannah's recipe. I just followed it down to the letter, that's all."

"Oh, you're too modest." Mrs. Jessup shook her head. "No matter the recipe, the food comes together differently depending on the cook. And Mr. Harbin is right, it was delicious. If we're all finished, let's take a walk in the cool night air, shall we?"

Everyone immediately began to move. Simon was the last one up, glancing around the room before skirting a shy glance at Miss Foster again. Would he have a chance to talk with her? Clearly that's why the Jessups had invited him over, but he couldn't help wondering what the young lady was thinking as well. Did she know why he was there? Did she care?

The Jessups had linked up arms, as had the Harbins. With them already down the lane, it was just Simon and Olivia on the porch, standing apart and wondering if they should follow. He put out his arm with a smile, hoping she would take it.

In the light of their lantern, she hesitated as she gazed up at him with a curious expression. "Thank you," she said at last, and slipped her arm through his. She had a gentle touch, and his heart hammered as they started down the path. Simon tried to think of something to say, hoping he wouldn't ruin this evening.

Chapter Seven

She could see the hesitation in the handsome stranger and didn't blame him. It had been a while since she had been around another man like this. In fact, there had only ever been Jack for her, and it seemed like they'd had a lifetime together. Though he'd only been gone these last five months, the fact that they hadn't been married almost made this easier. Swallowing down the fear and the pain, Olivia offered him a smile. "Nice evening for a walk."

They entered the lane and the two of them trailed slowly behind the other couples. "Yes, it's a lovely night, indeed," Simon answered after a moment of hesitation.

She glanced at him, almost surprised to find he was looking upwards, and not at her. His gaze had reached her often enough, after all, throughout the meal. Taking a deep breath, she looked around them out of habit and then up at the sky.

"Would you look at that? I can see Orion."

She pointed to the sky, and then he did the same. "And there's Pegasus."

Impressed, Olivia raised her eyebrow at him. "You know your constellations?"

He was quiet, but the man was passionate about his interests. "I do, yes. Sometimes I worked at night as a child on the tracks with my father, you see. He'd help me stay awake by focusing on the stars. I'd search for each and every one of them. He taught me to track their movements through the seasons."

Nodding in fascination, Olivia glanced back up. "Oh, my favorite. Cassiopeia. She's still up there. My grandmother had a hard time sleeping, you see, so the two of us would keep odd hours. Especially in the winter, with the cold. We would get wrapped up in our blankets and snuggle up on the bench outside, trying to beat each other to find each of them. They're lovely, aren't they? Almost like…"

"Guardian angels?"

She turned to him thoughtfully, for the exact same thing had been on her mind. Giving Mr. Simon James a good look over, Olivia pondered on the man. "Exactly." She nodded, and they started to walk again.

The advert had been clear, that the boarding house accepted young ladies who wanted to come to Colorado for a new life. The basics of a new life for a woman in need included a husband. Susannah had broached the topic once she was well rested and settled in. While the conversation was still warm, there was much they hadn't spoken of and little that Olivia felt clear about.

But she realized, she was enjoying Mr. James' company.

"What do you do then, when you're not counting the stars?" Her curiosity was real and the question wasn't just meant to make polite conversation. For some reason, she hoped that came through. "Mrs. Jessup said you worked on the trains?"

He nodded. "On them, around them, under them—all of that. It's what the country needs, after all, with everyone starting to travel more. And especially with people coming west. It's nice to be needed somewhere. Sometimes I just manage folks, or sometimes I do the dirty work myself. I like working with my hands, even if the smell isn't always pleasant." There was a deep throated chuckle and Olivia could tell he was growing comfortable just as she was. "But it's been good to me, I suppose."

Olivia smiled and appreciated his hard-working attitude. That was one of the measures of a good man.

"When I'm not doing that, I'm with my sister on her husband's ranch. I help out with the animals, and I play with her kids. She's got a daughter, Frances. That little girl seems to be able to run nearly as fast as a horse. Then there's little Patrick. He has the loudest laugh. You can hear him across the fields. Such a happy child. Ah, they're good kids." He smiled and paused. "Sorry, I'm rambling."

She noticed that they had gone a good distance around the garden and the barn, and the trail was leading them back to the houses. Wrinkling her nose, Olivia wondered if the night was already coming to an end. "No, of course not. Your family sounds lovely, Mr. James. And you clearly care for them."

"I do. And please, call me Simon."

"Then you may call me Olivia," she grinned at him. She could feel him gazing at her now. Again. Her heart thumped and it took all her strength not to look up at him. This brought butterflies to her stomach, and that caught her by surprise. Only Jack had been able to cause that feeling. Pulling her coat closer, she focused on the path and tried to think of something to say.

Yet they walked in silence for several minutes, a peaceful quiet where she listened only to the beating of her heart. "It looks as though the evening has come to an end," he spoke as they reached the porch. "I'd best be on my way, I'm afraid."

Finally she looked up, seeing the Harbins were saying their goodbyes to the Jessups. They had already walked the trail, to her surprise. "Oh, right. It is late, after all. Thank you. Tonight was lovely, and I enjoyed your company. It's nice to find someone who enjoys the stars as much as I do," she added thoughtfully.

"Indeed," he was quick to return her smile. "Good night, then."

"Good night." Olivia slipped her arm out of his, feeling the chill set in before she wrapped her arms around herself. "It was nice to meet you, Simon." She turned towards the porch as she heard him clear his throat. So she turned back, and cocked her head, waiting.

It took him a minute, but finally he took a deep breath and offered a shy smile. "Is there any chance— I mean would you like some company later this week? I'd like to visit again, if you don't mind."

"I wouldn't mind at all. Friday?" She bit her lip waiting on his reply.

"Friday." He nodded. And after a second rush of farewells, the man was gone.

She helped clean up the supper dishes and then Ol-

ivia went to her room. As she dressed for bed and buried
herself beneath the covers, she considered the evening's
events and pondered on what this meant. She decided
to downplay it all. There was no reason to be excited
about making a new friend. She wasn't ready for anything more. He probably wasn't thinking about anything
other than friendship, so all would be well.

Chores and her other assorted duties kept her busy
during the week. She was learning to cook lately, and
that took most of her control. By the time Friday arrived, she had completely forgotten until Susannah reminded her that she was cooking for four that evening.

"We have a guest?" she asked in confusion.

The woman laughed. "Yes. Or rather, you do. Isn't
Mr. James joining us, upon your invitation?"

She flushed in embarrassment. "Oh, right. Yes, of
course. Oh!" Then she looked down at her own clothes
and realized they were rather dirty, having spent the
morning picking vegetables out of the garden.

It wasn't the prettiest sight, and Olivia bit her lip. She
couldn't possibly be seen by Simon like this. Sighing,
she looked up hopefully at Susannah and clasped her
hands. "Do you mind if I…?"

Susannah shook her head and waved her off. "Of
course, of course. Go right along, dear. I'll set the table.
Don't be long, though. The men are most likely on their
way."

Heart hammering, the young woman bustled off to
her room. Her hand fluttered around her face as she
pinched her cheeks and brushed her hair again, wish-
ing it would decide to either stay curled or stay straight,

not in between. Once she was in her nicest dress, she fluffed up the edged lace then looked in her mirror.

She hadn't dressed up nicely like this for a while now. Touching her dress, Olivia considered how she looked, and thought of Jack. His dashing smile, that dark hair falling across his forehead. She stopped, and considered it for a moment. After blinking several times, she tried to drag him away from her thoughts, and think of Simon instead. It took her several minutes, trying to bring the quiet man to mind. The pattering in her heart faded away with Jack, and eventually she made her way back to the kitchen. She didn't want to be late.

Susannah was right that the men were near. Olivia had just finished setting the fresh bread on the table when the women heard the door open and found the two men strolling inside. The taller man moved confidently around the table over to his wife, where the long-haired blonde woman welcomed his embrace and accepted a kiss on the forehead. Olivia dropped her gaze modestly, but peeked over to Simon.

He was glancing at her as well so she hurriedly looked away, trying not to smile. He looked just as she recalled, but was smiling a little brighter than before. Dinner went well, as Susannah and Lucas drew them both into the conversations. Simon was funny, Olivia learned, and had enough jokes about his failures, his success, and his sister's family that kept her cheeks hurting and heart light all evening.

After they finished eating, Simon joined Olivia on the porch, and they watched the stars come out. She wrapped her shawl closer around her as he adjusted their blanket carefully, and sighed. "It's a lovely crescent moon, isn't it?"

"It is," he agreed. "Last night, I took my niece and nephew out to the mountains. It was rather warm for March, you see, and I bundled them in blankets and we had a wonderful view of the stars. We saw a shooting star, too, just before we returned home. You would have liked it, I think."

She nodded thoughtfully. "I think so, yes. Your niece and nephew are very lucky to have you. I would have loved to have seen that shooting star. I've only ever seen one or two."

He chuckled, shaking his head. "They're fun children. Next time, I'll be sure to bring you."

The idea made her heart flutter. He sounded so sure of a next time, of a future. Olivia's gaze dropped. They were already nearly touching, and she could feel his warmth. He was so close. Swallowing, she tried to think of something to say. What did she even want him to know? Olivia realized she wasn't sure what she wanted either. Wrinkling her nose, it took her a minute to consider her options.

"I would like that," she said at last, and looked over to find him watching her thoughtfully. He was already smiling, and she returned it willingly. "Very much," she added.

Chapter Eight

Friday suppers at the Jessups became a tradition for Simon. After the delicious meal, he would enjoy some time with the couple and most particularly with Miss Olivia Foster. They spent a fair amount of time on the porch watching the stars in the sky, talking quietly. She had a soft-spoken voice, one that reminded him of a trickling stream in summer. And she had been a nurse, so she had all sorts of intriguing stories to share, ones that made her tear up and ones that made him laugh.

A friendship bloomed as they grew comfortable in each other's presence. He looked forward to Fridays more than any other day, and found himself one Tuesday not wanting to wait until the end of the week to see Olivia again. Besides, Simon had a new shirt to wear and no work for the day. After gathering his courage, he took two horses and gathered some food before heading over to the boarding house.

"Oh." Olivia's eyes widened in delight when she opened the door for him. "Simon. What are you doing here today?"

Taking a deep breath, he shrugged. "I thought perhaps you might like to join me for lunch? Unless you're busy, of course?" He hadn't thought of that. So focused on creating a delightful surprise for her, Simon suddenly was unsure of this idea he'd gone straight ahead with and not considered anyone else's situation.

The young lady looked behind her down the hall, thinking. Her soft red hair was curled around her face, left down and trailing down her back. She wore an apron with flowers on it, and there was flour or sugar on her face, but he couldn't tell which. And then when she turned to face him again, she was wearing an even brighter smile than before. "I'd love to. I'm sorry, do come in. Take a seat, and I will return shortly, if that's all right with you?"

He nodded eagerly, watching her hopefully. "Yes, yes of course. Wonderful." Obediently he followed her into the sitting room, taking off his hat and sitting on the edge of his seat. He wanted to say something more, but she waved and hurried off. It was an excruciating seven minutes of waiting, but he endured it for her.

"Where are we off to?"

Her presence caught him off guard and he hastily clambered up to his feet, breathless. She had cleaned the white powder off her face, left behind the apron, and even pulled her hair back. Olivia Foster was like a fresh breath of air and he gasped for it. "I, um—I found a spot just two miles closer to town, by the stream… it made me think of you, so maybe that's a good place for lunch." He shrugged and offered a smile. "I'd like to take you there, if you like."

Following him to the door she picked up her coat. "I see. Sounds lovely."

He led her to the wagon and helped her up, wrapping them both in blankets to start on their way. Olivia told him about her day so far as Simon drove them along, and soon enough they landed at their destination.

Olivia sighed with a smile as she looked around. "Oh, this is lovely, indeed. Look at this view! Unbelievable. Simon, this really is exquisite." She looked over at him with a cheerful smile and he stopped, soaking it all in until she turned away. His cheeks flushed and he hurried around to help her down. They dug in, talking and laughing as they were lately prone to do.

When they finished with lunch, Olivia jumped to her feet. "We should take a walk. It's a lovely day. The sun is shining so brightly and I just love it. Shall we?"

He hastened to his feet, wrapping up the food and then joining her. Simon offered her his arm, and she carefully looped hers through his as they started off walking. Here in the hills was where the snow had gathered though it was more than he had expected. Their feet sloshed through the soggy ground and it made him chuckle. "I'm afraid I haven't exactly brought you somewhere dry."

Olivia looked over and grinned. "It is rather unfortunate." Her voice was almost playful as she giggled. "But fabric dries and mud can be washed out. It's days like this that matter more, don't you think?"

He pretended to think about it and nodded. "Apparently you're not a prissy city girl who gets cranky at the drop of a hat. I like it." Then he laughed.

"What do you mean? I may have taken to life out

away from the city, but I still have standards, Simon James." She put her hands on her hips and stared at him with an unwavering glare.

For a moment, Simon was worried he'd offended her. Then he saw her straight face give way to a smile. Finally, she laughed out loud, stepped forward and pushed him into a patch of mud just a step to his left.

"Ach! What did you just do?" He stepped out of the mud and started wiping his shoes on the drier grass when he finally found some.

Olivia took a step back and then another. She had pulled her shawl over her face but he could still see the mirth in her eyes.

"You think I can't see you laughing at me? And this is how it's going to be?" Shaking his head, he marched towards her.

She squealed and darted away from him. Simon saw the flush of her cheeks and something tingled down his spine. He hurried after her, trying to avoid as much mud as he could.

They chased each other back and forth for several minutes until in their haste, they ran into each other by a large oak tree. Olivia slipped and grabbed Simon's arm but he slipped up as well, only managing to keep her from falling under him. He hit the ground hard with Olivia on top of him now. He didn't even feel the stab of pain from hitting the ground.

She cried out in his ear, but it was cut short as she landed on him, clutching his arms tightly. Olivia caught his gaze and they stared at each other breathlessly, and suddenly all he could hear was how loud his heart was beating. Surely, she could hear it out in all this silence?

Simon looked up at her, those pretty freckles across her face and those sparkling green eyes.

That's when he realized that the tingling he had felt along his spine so often lately, was telling him how much he wanted to see what it was like to kiss Miss Olivia Foster.

As he brushed a little smear of dirt off her cheek, his thumb brushed against her lips and he couldn't wait any longer. His lips found hers, and for a minute he was certain he'd never tasted anything sweeter.

Until they pulled away, and Olivia's eyes widened as Simon suddenly realized what was happening. "Oh dear," she murmured, and scrambled to her feet. The cold air wrapped around him instantly and Simon stared at the sky, wondering if that kiss had really just happened. He thought his heart would pound its way right out of his ribs. Pulling himself to sit up, he swallowed and looked as Olivia drew away.

Her cheeks were bright red, much more colorful than her hair. Biting her lip, the young woman wasn't looking at him, but fiddling with her shawl. She looked anxious and nervous, just as he felt inside. The moment had made him feel so warm, but now something grew unsettled within him, and he hurried to his feet. Simon thought carefully as he wiped the mud off his clothes as best he could, and managed a smile, albeit slightly unsteady.

Awkwardness in the quiet started to settle in, and he wanted to break it immediately. "You look cold," he offered finally. "Perhaps it was time I took you home." He didn't mean it, not really. They hadn't even eaten.

But Simon didn't know what else to say, and she looked anxious.

"Perhaps," she replied, and nodded sharply. "I think that might be a good idea."

He swallowed. She drew closer so they could walk back to their spot, but not enough that they would touch. Simon considered holding out his arm to her, especially since she stumbled twice, but now he was too shy. They were quiet as he cleaned things up and took her home. When he returned to his sister's, Simon talked little before retiring early to bed.

That night, Jane came to him in his dreams. He could see the short, dark-haired woman standing by the window, watching the sunrise. "Isn't it nice?" And she turned to him, her eyes dark. "But you never talk to me anymore."

"What do you mean, darling?" He reached for her, but for some reason, Simon couldn't reach her. He walked and he walked, but Jane was never close enough. "Jane? Jane! What do you mean?" He put out a hand, grabbing for her. The floorboards were slick beneath his feet, and he knew he was moving. Perspiration broke out across his forehead, and he started to run. But she never grew any closer.

"You're never around. Don't you care about me anymore?" Her voice reverberated through his bones, shaking him to the core so hard that he woke up in a cold sweat. Simon gasped for breath, looking around to find he was still in the barn. Jane wasn't there, but dead. She wasn't coming back.

Simon could feel her presence there, everywhere, and his thoughts turned back to that kiss with Olivia.

A cold feeling of dread slipped down his spine as it all came to him. He had kissed another girl. A girl who wasn't Jane. What was he doing?

Biting back a sob, he buried his head in his hands. How could he hurt Jane like this? How could he be such a fool?

Chapter Nine

Susannah had hot sweet apple cider ready by the time she heard the wagon making its way up to the house. Peeking out the window, she saw Simon and Olivia sitting there together, wrapped in blankets, and hopefully closer than when they had left. She couldn't tell for sure. Her heart thumped excitedly as she grinned, eager to see how the picnic had went.

It had been a spontaneous activity, not one that she had come up with or suggested. But she had written it down in her notebook for the next time, and her notes included other ideas of bringing the couple together.

Turning back to the room, she rubbed her hands together to ensure the place looked cozy enough. Bustling around, Susannah brought out another thick blanket, and then brought over a few filled mugs, steaming and filling the room with a delicious smell. Then she backed away, smiling and satisfied. That's when the door opened.

"There you two are," Susannah started, but turned to find only Olivia there, shivering as she pulled off her muddy boots. The blonde paused, peeking out the window to see Simon and his cart headed down the lane already, just a small figure in the distance. Why hadn't he come in, she wondered. Disappointed, she turned back to Olivia, wondering if she had missed something. "Oh. He's leaving already?"

"I'm afraid so. I'm sorry, Susannah, but I'm quite chilled and would like to find warmer clothes. Do you mind if I lie down for a while?"

Susannah stepped out of her way. "Oh, I see. Yes, yes, of course." She nodded, and put out a hand. "Are you all right? Is everything—"

Olivia nodded, stepping back. "Just fine." But she kept her head low and sniffled. "I'll try to return to help with supper." And then she headed off to her room in the boarding house without another word or look back.

Dropping her hand, Susannah glanced at the muddy shoes uncertainly and worried about what she had missed. Back to the fireplace she went, taking one of the blankets and a mug of cider to enjoy as she tried to think this through. Perhaps she needed to be present for more occasions in the beginning. Maybe the two of them weren't ready to be on their own yet.

As a third party, there was only so much she could do for the matchmaking process, she knew, but surely she could still be of help. The only problem was that she needed to understand the situation in order to provide any assistance. If only Olivia would tell her what was going on. If she would share what she was thinking.

"You're thinking too hard again, aren't you?"

She looked up, gripping her mug tightly, and found Lucas standing there. Of course. Trying to hide her surprise, she shrugged and took another sip. But he knew everything and gave her a small smirk before grabbing his own cup of cider and sitting down next to her. Susannah tossed some of her blanket onto his lap as he kissed her forehead. "It's giving you forehead wrinkles. They're cute, but they look heavy," he explained. "What's on your mind today, Susie darling?"

Pouting, she gave him a look. "Relationships are difficult. Well, other people's relationships are," she amended at his raised eyebrow. "Things have been going well, haven't they? Between Olivia and Simon? But she just came home without a word, and he didn't even bring her to the door. I don't understand it."

Lucas settled into his seat by wrapping an arm around her shoulder. She rested her head on him, staring into her nearly finished mug. It was delicious, but it was supposed to be for the couple. She'd even put extra sugar in to make sure it was especially sweet. Trying to think her way through this problem to a solution without all the details was particularly difficult, and she just wasn't sure what to do about it.

When she finally turned to ask Lucas what he thought about the situation, Susannah found him dozing off. Hurriedly she grabbed his cup before it could spill, and carefully set both mugs back on the table. Chuckling quietly, she stood up and wrapped the blanket snug around him and yawning herself, headed to the kitchen. Perhaps starting supper would help her to focus.

Susannah set the table and had finished preparing supper by the time Lucas woke up. He gave her an abashed smile before washing up. Giggling, she brought the cornbread to the table and tossed him a towel for his hands. After years of being together, they often didn't need to say a word in order to help one another. Their familiarity was a comfort, and she liked how he found small ways to touch her elbow, her hand, her shoulder as she moved around the kitchen.

They said grace, but she didn't eat. Instead, she saw the empty spot beside them and frowned. What should she do about Olivia? She had yet to find herself an answer. "Eat," Susannah told Lucas at last. "I want to check on Miss Foster."

Before she went, she picked up a warm mug of cider and headed for the boarding house. Susannah made her way over to Olivia's room, and knocked quietly twice. When she didn't hear an answer, she knocked again but a little louder. After a minute, she heard a rustling of sheets and Olivia stuck her head through the doorway all blurry-eyed.

"Oh, I'm sorry." Olivia managed a smile. "Is it already supper time?"

She looked flushed and had dark circles around her eyes. It almost looked as though she had been crying. Susannah's brow creased as she studied the young woman's face, wondering what was going on inside her mind. "Yes," she said slowly. "I brought you cider in case you weren't hungry, however. How are you doing?"

"F-fine," she stammered, accepting the mug but keeping the door nearly shut. "Thank you."

"And you're sure you're fine?" Susannah put a hand on the door as it started to close. "Are you positive? You just…you don't seem the same. Since you came back this afternoon, you seem withdrawn. I'm a bit worried about your wellbeing. That's all."

Olivia swallowed, glancing down at the mug in her hand. "I'm fine, of course," she murmured in a hollow voice. "I'm just tired. It was…very chilly today."

The door slowly closed and Susannah was left alone again. Frowning, she stared at the door for a solid minute or two before grudgingly turning back towards the kitchen and Lucas. When she arrived, she sat and stared at her plate for several minutes. Lucas looked at her frequently, but wisely chose not to say anything until finally Susannah sighed and rested her chin in both her hands.

"Maybe I was a fool to do any of this," she said at last. "I don't feel as though I understand anything at all."

That made Lucas laugh and Susannah could only glare at him. "You're taking this much too seriously," he told her, putting a piece of pie on her plate. "I told you that you were thinking about this too much. It's probably nothing. I'm sure she's like you."

"What?" Susannah objected. "I don't act like that."

His pointed look said otherwise. "It's hard to get the truth from you sometimes. You don't like to say what's in your heart because you don't want to hurt other people."

She tried to consider what he was saying. "Do you think she doesn't like Simon, then, is that it?"

He shrugged. "I think something's going on that she doesn't want you to worry about. But when she's ready, she'll tell you. Remember, the road to love and trust isn't always a straight one."

Biting her lip, Susannah fiddled with her fork. He had a point, and now she could see it. His words made some sense. Since the young woman arrived, she knew there was something going on with her. After the life she had survived, and she'd said something about needing to leave quickly, but never saying exactly what had happened. Something was on her mind, something was haunting her.

Sighing, Susannah leaned back in her seat and shook her head. Perhaps, then, the matchmaking business never got any easier.

Chapter Ten

Lying in her bed, Olivia opened her eyes again and stared at the ceiling. It was brown, because that was the color of wooden planks. Dark wooden brown planks. It was just a ceiling, after all. Something people didn't usually think about, not in Colorado. There were a lot of things they didn't consider. And there were a lot of thoughts she'd been ignoring. Like Jack.

Olivia Foster tried not to close her eyes, because that's where she would find him. Her heart pounded and her eye twitched. Her hands balled into fists. Every part of her body stiffened, but she couldn't resist blinking once, twice, and then she closed her eyes. There he was. Her muscles relaxed.

"I'm sorry," she whispered, heaving a sigh. "Jack."

Her fingers traced over her lips, and they felt warm. She could still feel his own brush against hers as if it was happening all over again. Olivia started and opened her eyes again. It kept happening. Simon kept happening. And Jack. One man within her mind only and so far away, and one man nearly within reach.

Clasping her shaking hands together, she tried to do the same to her thoughts. Heart pounding, she tried to figure this out. What was she to do? Even though she had come so far, and even though she had known what staying at the Jessup Boarding House meant, Olivia hadn't thought as far as this situation.

What had she expected? A safe place, a harbor from her last home. Anything was better than Vermont, she knew that much. She looked at her hands. In their normal state, they were so calm and so steady. She could stitch like no other, on a pillowcase or bodice. Olivia was an excellent nurse, and she cared for sick people better than anything else. When she worked with the doctor, her mind was focused and she knew her next move no matter the situation. And now, she didn't know where to turn or who to turn to.

"I promise," she could recall Jack saying to her. "I promise you'll enjoy it. Please, come with me?"

It had been a beautiful day, and she had looked outside around him. The sun was shining and the sky was so blue. Of course she had the urge to run and jump, but that wasn't something she'd done in years, not since she was a little girl. Olivia's heart had pattered at the thought, but even more at spending an afternoon with Jack.

He'd been a nice young man, one who had looked out for her often. They lived on opposite sides of town, and he'd been to the nicer school growing up. But often they found each other at church, and sometimes even during their errands. She recalled the time he'd sprained his wrist. He came to the doctor's office while Dr. Hadley had been out to lunch. Instead of asking him to wait, she'd wrapped it and advised him to keep from using it for a week.

"You promise? How do you know for sure I'll enjoy an outing?" That afternoon she couldn't imagine how he could guarantee her happiness. Biting her lip, she'd wiped her hands on her apron. It had been a Sunday so the clinic was closed. She'd just set a pie down to cool, and Grandmother was resting. There was nothing for her to do, and Jack had showed up.

After that, he started coming to her for other things, besides his sprained wrist. Apparently Jack had his share of accidents, usually small cuts or bee stings or sometimes a bruise he wanted her to look at. It made her laugh, but she loved the way he smiled at her.

Sometimes when he'd shown up with a scratch that needed cleaning, he'd bring flowers he'd claimed to find on the road. The man had the prettiest eyes and darkest hair. While he wasn't very tall, it was nice to look straight into his eyes. And unlike the others in town, he didn't mind her height.

Jack's promise had been enough for her. She'd pulled the apron off carefully, setting it down before accepting his arm and went out the door. He'd led her into the sunshine with that wide open grin, leading her down the street. They'd walked for hours, playing in the stream and talking and plucking flowers for her Grandmother.

That had become a Sunday tradition, Jack stopping over to say hello to her and take her for a walk. Even in the snow, he would be there for her. Soon he was joining them for supper, and visiting her daily at the doctor's clinic. Eventually, Jack knew Olivia better than she knew herself, and always knew what to say around her.

"What do I do without you?" Now, she sat up on her bed and stared out towards the window. Even in this new place with friendly people, she was still alone. Staring back down at her hands, Olivia frowned. Simon James had kissed her, and it had felt nice. But it was too fast, too soon. What about Jack? He was gone, but she had to honor his memory. She needed to honor his precious memory.

No matter what solution came to mind, it scared her. What was someone to do when they lost their soulmate? She was still so young, and with a bleak future ahead of her. Sighing, Olivia rubbed her eyes and jumped as there was a knock at her door.

Her tongue stuck to the roof of her mouth as she carefully slid onto her feet, trying to convince herself there was no reason to be so nervous. There was no one chasing her, and there never had been. Taking a deep breath, Olivia brushed her hair back and cracked the door open. "Y-yes?"

It was Susannah, of course. Because no one else would be there. The blonde cocked her head with a bright smile, clearly unbothered, and held up the muffin in her hand. "Good morning, dear. Are you hungry? You never came out for supper last night. Are you ill?"

"Just a bit under the weather," Olivia said finally, offering a tight smile. "But thank you." She hesitated, and then grudgingly accepted the muffin. Her stomach growled and she realized that Susannah was right. It had been a while since she'd eaten. She hadn't eaten at the picnic, nor had she eaten any supper. But at the memory, something in her made her freeze.

The other woman noticed. "Is there anything I can do to help? Olivia, there's a lot on your mind, isn't there?"

Olivia's throat tightened. "I don't know what you can do."

Susannah's big blue eyes were so kind, so inviting. Olivia sighed. The other woman had a strength beyond what Olivia might have supposed. Leaning against the doorframe, she stared at the floor as she held the muffin.

"Come on." Susannah invited herself into the room, leading Olivia back to the bed. The two women sat on the edge and the other woman found a hairbrush that she started using on Olivia's hair. The motions were firm and slow, just like her Grandmother's. She felt her muscles relaxing, and she sighed again, oddly comforted. But this time, it was lighter. "What's on your mind, dear?"

Looking at her hands, Olivia swallowed. "How do you know you're doing the right thing? I'm just so confused. Things were going well, but I'm so far away from everything I know, Susannah."

It took the woman a while to speak. "You're never truly sure, not until afterwards. I'm afraid that's the way faith works, Olivia. You pray and you listen for His voice. You hope what you think you hear is the right thing. Your faith that the Lord will guide you has to be true. If you feel peace, then it means that it's right. And if not, then you'll know that, too."

Rubbing her eyes, Olivia tried to decipher the meaning. "But…but what if both are terrifying notions?"

Susannah offered a light chuckle, patting Olivia's shoulder. "I'm afraid that's just the way life is sometimes. Now, when I first arrived here in Colorado, I was scared and I was alone. I didn't know where I was or if I was in the right place. All I knew was that I'd wanted to leave Boston and it felt right that I came here."

Olivia blinked quickly, taking in Susannah's words.

"Lucas is a good man. He's strong, protective, and funny. When I first met him, I had no idea what to think, or what I was getting myself into. He's still very much a Ranger at heart, and I don't always understand him. When we were married, I was scared of every step that followed."

Olivia turned to her. "Then when did you know it was right?"

Returning the brush, Susannah slid off the bed and flattened her skirts. A soft, thoughtful look spread across her face, showing off a small sprinkling of freckles she had earned from the sun. "One morning, I woke up and went out onto the porch. I don't remember exactly when—it could have been a week, a month, or a year after we wed. The sun was just rising, and I could hear the birds singing in the trees. And the sweetest breeze touched my hair. It was like an angel," she chuckled, shaking her head as though it were funny. "Like an angel telling me I was right where I needed to be."

Glancing at the brush, Olivia pondered on this. "Do you think I'll know, too? Someday?"

"Someday soon," Susannah patted her knee with a nod. "Soon, I'm sure."

Chapter Eleven

It took him a good hour to climb out of bed that morning. Every move only exhausted his efforts and Simon considered going back to bed. Sighing, he leaned out the window and glanced at the sun that had long since risen. He had never stayed down for so long. The heat warmed his bones, and it took the rest of his strength to move away from the window.

After tending to the cows, Simon headed to the house. It smelled good, biscuits and gravy they must have had for breakfast. Carefully he pulled off his shoes and washed his hands, listening to his sister moving around the kitchen.

"What's wrong?" Lillian noticed his swollen down-turned gaze the moment he entered the kitchen. His sister was perceptive like that. "Simon, what is it?"

Glancing around the house, he sighed and rubbed his face once again. Was it so easy to notice? Leaning against the wall, he tried to collect himself. From the looks of it, her husband was already out in the fields and the children were outside playing.

"Simon?" She tugged on his arm, leading him to the table where they sat down and she touched his face delicately, checking for a fever. "You're warm but you're not that warm. Did you get any sleep?"

He shrugged. "Some." Then he tried to summon up a smile for her, telling her not to worry. "I'm fine, I just…"

When he didn't say anything else for a good minute, Lillian brushed her hair away and came up with another topic. "How did the picnic go yesterday with Olivia? I didn't see you after you came back. Did the two of you enjoy your time together? And how was the food?"

But he hesitated, because he wasn't sure about the answer. He didn't know what to say, not even about the basket sitting in the barn by his bed. "It started out really well," Simon managed finally, and then stared at his hands on the table. "But I'm not certain about anything else, I'm afraid."

"No," Lillian frowned. "Surely it wasn't as terrible as you thought?"

"We kissed."

She blinked quickly, clearly not having expected that detail. He could feel her gaze on him, both of her hands still covering one of his, and she squeezed but still Simon refused to meet his sister's gaze. Lillian chuckled awkwardly after a second. "Well, isn't that a good thing?"

"I don't know," he tried to explain, attempting to put his thoughts and feelings into words for his sister and for himself. He wasn't sure there was any way to explain what had happened, on the picnic or in his dreams. "I thought so, in the moment. But then she pulled away like she was unhappy. And then I dreamed of Jane. Oh, Jane. She was so far away. I'm not trying to forget her. Am I?" He couldn't decide.

His sister shook her head. "No! Not at all. Simon, she wouldn't want you to be sad and lonely. Jane would have wanted you to be happy, more than anything. She wouldn't want you to be miserable. Trying to live again isn't the same thing as trying to forget her."

"She's only been gone two years. I still wake up thinking she will be right there."

She squeezed his hand again. "You're feeling guilty, and that's normal. But what's not normal is how you're treating yourself. Jane wouldn't want this for you and I don't want it for you either. I'm sure no one else does, including Olivia. Now I'm sure she was just shy, or something like that."

"I don't know." He looked off out the window for a moment as he gathered his thoughts. "She didn't talk to me for the whole ride back to her house."

Slipping away, Lillian left his side. He listened to her knocking around dishes until she brought him over a plate filled with two biscuits covered in gravy and a mug of coffee. She put a fork in his hand that rested on the table. "You're not thinking straight," she instructed in a firm tone, one that she usually only reserved for her children. "Now eat."

A flicker of a smile graced his lips before he nodded obediently and cut a bite and put it into his mouth. It melted in his mouth and he felt like he was able to breathe again. He hadn't realized how hungry he was and it helped him gain focus, putting food in his stomach. "These are mighty good," he murmured between another bite as he pulled the plate closer.

She chuckled. "Good. And perhaps while you eat, you'll listen to me?" He shrugged and she poked his shoulder. "I mean it. Simon, your time with Olivia has made you happy. I haven't seen you this way in a long time, not since Jane. I even heard you whistling the other day. Just because she seemed uncertain about the kiss, it doesn't mean she doesn't like you."

He looked up at her, shook his head, and looked down at his plate.

"After all, it doesn't sound like you're reacting quite well to the kiss either. Perhaps she had similar concerns? You said she told you about several tragedies in her past, and maybe she's worried about what will happen. She came here so recently, and everything's new to her. She's probably in the same boat you are, Simon."

He paused. "She mentioned there had been someone else." His brow furrowed as he tried to remember. What had Olivia said? It was someone she was courting, or a fiancé in Vermont, but something had happened so she had needed to leave. Twiddling his fork, he tried to think this through. "But what about Jane?"

Lillian gave him a pointed look. "Jane will always be a part of you, but she's gone. You know she'll always be in your heart. And Olivia would understand that. She will be a part of you in the best way. And it's okay to have a new start with someone new. Jane would want you to be happy."

He let silence settle in. Listening to the thudding of his heart, Simon tried to think about this. After a minute, Lillian must have decided she'd said enough and stood up, moving around the kitchen. She set the table, and went to check on the children.

Once the kitchen was cleaned and bread was rising for the supper meal, Lillian touched her brother's shoulder. "You need to get up and get moving," she instructed him. "Go work in the fields and think about what I said, all right?"

"All right," he said vaguely, nodding absently as he clambered up to his feet. "All right." Pulling his boots on, Simon put his hat on and made his way into the sunshine. Like that first bite that morning, the light brought him clarity and he started working through his troubled thoughts out in the fields.

Frank was a quiet man, a hard worker focused on his efforts. Though the two of them worked closely to one another, neither of them said a single word. But it was good, Simon knew, and his sister was right. That little girl he used to watch over had definitely grown up into a wise woman.

By midafternoon, he realized he was being a fool. Lillian was right. He could be happy again, and he had learned lately that this was possible. Jane was out of reach now, but it didn't mean that she had to disappear. And it meant that he could be happy again, with Olivia.

It put a new outlook on life for him, the moment that Simon realized what a fool he had been. Scaring himself out of this opportunity, scaring himself away from love. And he was certain that Olivia Foster felt the same, that she was hesitant to begin again as he was. Just like that, he felt new life breathed into him and he could hardly focus on his task anymore. With a new drive, he couldn't just stand there feeding the goats now. No, he had to do something about it.

Simon dropped everything and headed towards the barn. He waved to Lillian as he passed, and then continued down the road. The wind took his hat, but it didn't matter anymore. Nothing mattered, except for seeing Olivia. He headed towards the Jessup home, his heart thudding more loudly than he could ever remember.

Chapter Twelve

"I'm perfectly fine," Susannah muttered to herself, glancing in her reflection again. She wrinkled her red nose, and that only made it hurt worse. Staggering a breath through her mouth, she pouted. After wrapping a blanket around her on top of the shawl, she turned away from the window and carefully made her way down to the kitchen to find something to do.

She had woken up with the foggiest head and worst stuffy nose of her life. Lucas and Olivia had convinced her to return to bed after breakfast, then the two of them headed off to town without her. She admitted to herself she didn't feel like leaving the house and was grateful for Olivia who by now knew exactly what they needed to stock the shelves.

It had only been an hour or so since they'd left, but Susannah was bored. Exhausted, aching, and bored. Shuffling to the table, she took a seat and looked around. After blowing her nose in an extra handkerchief, Susannah considered her options. She could make that loaf of bread they needed, sweep, or return to her bed. It was a hard decision, so she figured resting for another minute wouldn't matter.

There was a knock at the door that startled her. Susannah inhaled sharply, not realizing her eyes had been closed. Clumsily she pulled herself together and staggered towards the front door, leaning against the wall when she got there. There was a fresh breeze that only tickled her already swollen nose as she opened the door, and squinted into the light to find Simon standing there.

"Oh." Her eyes widened. "Good day, Simon. We weren't expecting you today, were we?" Furrowing her brow, she tried to think.

He nodded with a nervous smile before shaking his head, realizing it had been a question. "No, I'm afraid I came unexpectedly. I was hoping to speak with Olivia. I'm real sorry to barge in, Mrs. Jessup. I shouldn't be bothering you. Are you all right?"

He was polite, that's for certain. She knew she looked terrible, with her hair unkempt and shivering beneath her layers. Sighing, Susannah rubbed her head. "I've been better, that's for certain. Let's talk in the warmth of the sun, shall we?" She stepped out to the porch and into the sunlight.

It was much too bright, and for a moment she was blinded. Only with Simon's hand did she make it to the bench without falling over. "You look unwell." He frowned deeply. "Perhaps you should return to the house. I'll go get Mr. Jessup and maybe we can get you to the doc—"

She waved a hand in the air. "Honestly, I'm fine. There's nothing to fuss about. I'm under the weather, that's all. But let's talk. Right now, my husband and Olivia are taking care of some errands in town. It's about time you and I catch up with what's been happening."

The stiffness slipped from his shoulders, and only then did Susannah notice there was something different about him. There had been something on his mind, and she had thrown him off. Simon was trying to reorient himself, fiddling with his clothes as his eyes darted from her to the house to the road and back.

"Then, I can… I mean…" He looked away towards the barn clearly trying to put his words together.

"If you don't mind my asking, how did the picnic go? From your point of view?" Susannah decided to redirect the conversation since it didn't appear he knew where to take it. Sometimes men just needed guidance on where to start moving. "Olivia returned rather quiet, I thought."

Simon paused, and his eyes turned downward. "Yes. At first, it went well. We enjoyed each other's company and talked. But we got off track, I guess. You might recall that I was married before." He cut his eyes to her suddenly, his gaze intense on hers. "And I don't think I was really prepared for something new. Someone new."

Through the fog, Susannah began to see the intersecting pieces and the connections between everything. Olivia's fear and uncertainty, the doubt that lingered definitely matched the expression on Simon's face now. What she thought would bring them together wasn't working as she had hoped. Trying to get comfortable, she leaned back and sighed. "So the two of you respect one another, but are afraid to move on from those you loved before."

Grudgingly he nodded, and then turned to her. "Who was he? She was betrothed, right?"

"She didn't tell you the details?" Susannah hesitated, then went on when Simon gave a slight shake of his head. "Well, yes, she did lose the man she planned to marry. But if she didn't say more about it, I don't think it's my place to tell the story for her. But I can assure you, it is very similar to yours. Olivia Foster has faced a lifetime of loss. She has been left alone much too often and is worried she'll lose the next person she cares for. It makes sense that she'd believe that because of her past." With her hand wrapped up in the shawl, she patted the man's knee comfortingly. "She'll come around, though. I'm sure of it."

Simon took a deep breath and set his shoulders back. "Good. Because I want to marry her. It's why I came over."

For a moment, she didn't think she'd heard right. But the firmly set jaw and confidence in his gaze told Susannah that she had heard exactly what she thought she had. Heart beating, she sniffled and looked at him thoughtfully. "You mean it," she whispered. "You really mean it. You love her."

Laughing, Simon nodded and clambered up to his feet. Suddenly energized by this confession, the man started to pace on the porch and Susannah beamed. It was a precious moment, and she was so glad she wasn't missing this. The only thing missing was Olivia.

"I do," he said finally. "Yes, I mean it. I do love her. I love Olivia very much. This morning, I spoke with Lillian and she helped me see reason. We only have one life, and we need all the love we can find. Don't you think? And I know it's still soon, and we can wait if she wants, but if she'll have me, I want to marry that woman."

He stood tall and proud, and Susannah clapped from her seat. "I think—" but a coughing fit stopped her from finishing her thought. Clutching her chest, she fought for breath. Simon hurried to her side, patting her back as she gasped, finally drawing in fresh air.

"We should get you inside. Perhaps next week would be better for me to see Olivia."

She shook her head. "No, I don't want to be what keeps your relationship from progressing forward. Now, I'm sure I have some cider we can put over the fire. Let's get a few cups, and then we can start planning your proposal." She put out a hand and he carefully pulled her to her feet. "Surely you weren't just going to come out and say it, were you? Did you have anything more planned?"

"What else is there to say?" He frowned.

Susannah laughed as they headed inside. This new challenge gave her the energy she needed to pull together the nice hot cider for them. Holding a mug of the steaming drink spread warmth through her insides as she sat across from Simon who was trying to figure out how best to propose.

Sighing, Simon stared at his cup. "When I married Jane, she, well, we just knew it would happen. I don't think I ever actually asked her the question, we just decided that it was time. I actually think she just told me it was time. She was my closest friend, all through my childhood and all through the hardships and the joy. One day we were friends, one day we were closer, and the next we were married. Since our relationship was so easy. And different, I suppose…well, I never thought I would need to consider another." For a moment his expression went dark, and then he shook his head and offered Susannah a sheepish grin. "Do women really take the proposal seriously? How it's done, I mean?"

Chuckling, she shrugged. "Some take it seriously, and some don't. But it's an important thing to plan to be on the safe side. Now, let's see what we can come up with, shall we? Why, you could even stop back into town and go ask Olivia before the day is through!"

Now that was a thought. Susannah peered towards the windows. The weather was good and the sun was shining bright. Perhaps they would need to make their own trip to town.

Chapter Thirteen

"Flour, sugar. What else?" Olivia was nearly finished in the mercantile after stopping in the haberdashery and delivering some vegetables to the church. Pulling the scrap of paper from her pocket, she glanced over the errand list one more time. "Church and vegetables, haberdashery for buttons, then flour, sugar, and salt. That's what it was."

In a rather good mood, she started to hum as she waited for the supplies she needed. "Here we are," she beamed. "That should be everything."

The clerk took care of her list and found one of his errand boys to carry everything out to the wagon for her. Wrapping her coat around her, she followed the young man out, offering advice on the best way to put everything in place. "Perfect." She nodded when he was finished. "Thank you so much."

She watched the young boy, blushing and awkward, hurry back inside. Reaching for her bonnet, she started to put it back on. Today was a good day, and Susannah had been right about her needing to get out of the house. As Olivia turned to the front of the cart, she found Lucas headed in her direction. "There you are! I'm nearly finished. Oh, my." She was immediately concerned when she saw his troubled expression.

Dropping her hands to her side, she squinted at the man who came closer to her. Trouble, and guilt, and uncertainty. All of these emotions were ones Olivia had never seen in Lucas Jessup before, not in the few months that she had known him and his wife. If anything, he was much too calm and too confident most of the time.

"What is it?" She swallowed hard, not sure she wanted to hear what he would say.

"Let's go to my office." He took a deep breath, rubbing his forehead as he glanced around the street. He grabbed her arm when she didn't budge, but did so lightly, inviting her to join him down the block towards his sheriff's office. She hurried to keep up with him, wrapping her fingers around his arm in order to stay upright. Olivia noticed his eyes skirting the streets carefully, as though he were looking for something, or someone.

"But the wagon. We can't leave it." She was looking for any excuse she could think of to stall.

He shook his head. "It'll be fine. It all can wait." Normally Lucas wouldn't do such a thing. He never left anything unfinished. Swallowing, she found herself looking around the town carefully, wondering what was out there causing him to be so watchful. Dread filled her stomach and her mouth turned dry as the fear returned to her stomach. Just when she had thought it was finally fading, it came back like a tidal wave.

They reached his office, a small room with a desk.

It led off to one other room with a desk for Jeb Harbin, and then a back room with three cells. Lucas sat her down in his chair, and he started to pace the room. Olivia watched, twisting her hands in her lap, listening and waiting. Finally, she could bear the tension no longer.

"What's going on?" She asked finally, her voice just above a whisper. "Please, you're frightening me, Mr. Jessup."

At the sound of his name, he stopped. He hung his hat on the wall peg and finally brought out a folded piece of paper from his pocket. "We just received this in the mail. There were a few additional copies, but I've destroyed them."

"What are you talking about?" She frowned, confused as he handed her the crumpled paper. Carefully she unfolded it, only to have her heart bottom out at the sight of the document. It had a rough sketch of her and said *Wanted* in large red letters at the bottom. "What in the world?" Her jaw dropped in disbelief.

"You have a warrant out for your arrest," Lucas told her plainly. He leaned over on the desk, laying it out for her. "You're wanted across the States for the murder of a Jack Henderson." Her heart stopped. "And if you are found, you are to be apprehended and accompanied back to Vermont for trial."

She could feel the blood draining from her face, and the urge to faint was strong. Gasping for breath, Olivia tossed the paper back on the table and covered her mouth in horror. "No. No, please…"

Why would this be happening to her? She felt sick to her stomach, and though she wanted to run with every fiber of her being, she couldn't make her legs move.

Unable to stand on her own two feet, Olivia fell back into her chair.

Lucas looked at her with narrowed eyes and didn't say anything.

"Mr. Jessup, I swear, you have to believe me. I'm innocent, this is wrong!"

Her desperate plea caught his attention and he nodded, staring at the paper. For a minute she couldn't tell what he was thinking. She had no idea what he would do about this.

"That's what I thought. But Miss Foster, I need to know why this would be happening. I don't believe you could have hurt anyone, but you will need to tell me what happened in Vermont."

Tears were already trickling down her face. Sniffling, she tried to rub them away. But there were too many, just at the thought of her home. All the pain, all the hardships, what had it all been for?

"Jack Henderson was my betrothed." She sniffled loudly and fished in her reticule for a handkerchief. "When my grandmother died, his family took me in until we were married and could afford our own place. I had no place else to go. We were just saving as much money as we could. But there was an accident. It was a hunting accident. It had nothing to do with me, I swear it."

"Could anyone else have caused it?" he interrupted with a frown, thinking this through.

Her heart skipped a beat, trying to imagine that. "No." She shook her head at last. "No, it was an accident. He was separated from the group, you see, and there was nothing suspicious about it." She sniffled, shaking her head and trying to clear her thoughts.

"But they couldn't just turn me out to the streets, and I had nowhere else to go. Jack's uncle, Theodore, started plotting with Jack's mother about getting rid of me by marrying me off to someone else. Adam Parker, he was an untrustworthy businessman. Apparently the Henderson family would get paid if I married him. So I left. I left the moment I found out. But I swear, I haven't hurt anyone."

Mr. Jessup started pacing again. "How did you know about this? And about this deal with Mr. Parker?"

She shrugged. "Theodore wasn't a quiet man, no matter what he thought. And he complained enough about me using the family's money. I offered to leave once, but they knew how bad it would look on them. And everyone knew Mr. Parker, a cruel business man who traveled often, but I...well, I worked for the town's doctor, Dr. Hadley, you see, and I heard the stories. I knew the nasty things he did to people who crossed him." Shuddering at the memories, Olivia wiped away the tears and wondered how it had come to this. "Please, I'm not lying. I know I didn't share everything upfront, but I promise, this is everything I know. I thought it was over and I didn't want to worry anyone, I didn't want to be a bother. I just wanted to start over."

"I believe you," Mr. Jessup assured her. "However, this is a legal matter that must still be addressed. The fact that I have not put you behind bars means that I am not doing the duty I have sworn to the people of Rocky Ridge that I promised to do. So—" he offered her a tight smile "—I'm going to investigate this issue, and we're going to hide you away."

Her eyes widened. "Hide me? Whatever do you mean?"

After another minute of pacing, Lucas had it all figured out. Opening the desk, he pulled out a few dollar bills, and hurried her out of the station. "There's no time to pack, I'm afraid," he murmured in her ear as they headed down the street. "I'll have to tell Susannah. She's going to kill me. Fix your bonnet, put it over your eyes, will you?" She hurriedly obeyed. "Good. You're going on the stagecoach, and you get off at the next one. That'll be Berryville. Find a hotel to stay in, and keep your head down."

"I'm doing the best I can." She nodded and dipped her head further.

"I mean by not talking to people or going out or attracting attention. I can't make any promises, however, Olivia. You can stay there, or you can keep moving on. Once I get this taken care of, I can come there for you. Susannah and I won't begrudge you if you decide to keep moving on. You can write to us in a few months, and we can send you your things, if you like."

They had reached the stagecoach station. "What do you mean?" Olivia's heart thudded, staring at him.

Lucas sighed. "It means you can go anywhere and do anything. But right now, you just can't be here."

As she left town, riding away in the carriage, his words echoed in her mind. Her heart hammered and she tried to imagine leaving Rocky Ridge forever. And leaving Simon. She took a shaky breath and drew her cloak around her tighter, but kept her eyes wide open.

Chapter Fourteen

The cart wasn't that steady, with a wheel that wasn't well balanced. This made the cart tilt and it jolted every time they hit a small rut or rock in the road. Simon winced at a particularly rickety spot, and hurriedly glanced at the bundled up woman beside him. With one hand, she was holding onto the bench to stay upright, the other hand holding onto her blankets.

"Mrs. Jessup?" He cut his eyes over to her and then quickly back on the road in front of them.

She shook her head. "I'm fine, really, Simon. The air is doing me well. Don't you worry about me." Susannah smiled and reached out to touch his arm. "And you're doing me some good, as well. Honestly, it's just a cold." It was as though she sneezed just for effect.

Nodding, he decided to focus on the road then, unsure of what else to do with her. She had shown herself in the past to be a rather formidable woman in leading their dialogue and clearing the air between people. Now, he was mostly worried about getting in trouble with her husband for letting her join him in town. Shrugging it off, he tried to focus on his plans. On the other hand, perhaps Lucas would be able to talk some sense into her.

The two of them reached town soon enough, and they had errands to run. She was to go find Olivia and keep her from finding Simon shopping for the ring and the flowers and everything else. Simon started his errands by helping her off the wagon. "Can I be of any assistance? I don't want anything to happen to you."

Shaking her head, she grinned and fixed her hat. "What did I tell you? I'll be fine. I'm going to retrace Olivia's steps to find her. She should be at the haberdashery or the mercantile, I suppose, so I'll start there. And then I'll visit my husband at his office.

"You're welcome to either return the cart later today, or tomorrow if you get held up," she continued with a pointed gaze. "Now I want to make sure you get everything taken care of, do you understand? If you need anything, come find me or Lucas. Otherwise, we expect to see you at our house early Friday evening. Understood?"

Even if Lucas Jessup was sheriff, Simon doubted that even he could object under such a look as the one that Susannah gave him now. It was enough to send a man to the grave if he wasn't ready to obey. But he nodded, still wholeheartedly invested, and straightened with a grin. "I'll be there as soon as I can manage, ma'am."

"Good." She beamed, and bustled off with a sniffle.

Simon watched her wander off down the street, making sure she was all right. No one bothered her, but most people waved their greetings to her as she reached the haberdashery and entered, still upright with her head on straight. With a sigh of relief, he turned down the other direction of the street.

His first step was to Mr. Connelly's, an old friend of Frank Dane. Lillian and Frank had mentioned him before, in his consideration of settling here for good. Mr. Connelly was old in age, a loner who liked a good poker hand and constantly talked about getting enough money together to go to California. The one thing he always told everyone he had too much of, was land. One of the first folks in Rocky Ridge, the man had laid several claims to nearly half the town that he had been selling little by little over the years. Everyone knew it, and everyone went to him for property options.

Mr. Connelly grinned and wiped his face as he answered the door. "Mr. James! I had been wondering when I would have you come around. Do come in. Are you hungry?"

Confused at his words for having met the man for the first time, Simon slowly stepped in, pulling his hat off. "No, I'm very well, but thank you. What do you mean, you've been wondering?" Glancing around at the small house, suddenly he was wondering himself if he had come to the wrong place or if something was going on that he just didn't know about.

He followed the man to the kitchen where the man went back to eating greasy chicken thighs. It was a disgusting sight to watch, the liquid dripping from his fingers. Mr. Connelly looked rather a mess, but he looked satisfied and full. "Your family has mentioned you might be coming around in the next few months. Mr. Dane had me section off a nice parcel of land, just in case."

Pausing, Simon stared at him, speechless. He had thought it would be a lot more difficult than this. A few folks had once mentioned that they had had to argue and defend their needs for the land, to claim the land from him and why they needed it more than he did. The entire wagon ride into town, he had been working up his own need for the claim and preparing his argument. Now, the jumble of words filled his mind in a bushel and it was as though Connelly had just lit them on fire.

"Oh," he managed. He shook his head, trying to clear it, and attempted to say something else. Had Frank told him? He couldn't recall hearing of such a thing before, and he didn't know what to say. "Well then, that's great. I thought it might be more difficult than this."

Connelly gave off a booming laugh that made the table shake. Wiping his hands on his pants, the man stood. "Let me get the map and we can talk prices, shall we?" The man hummed a merry tune as he dug through his small desk and finally pulled out a hand drawn map. "I made this myself when I first arrived, you know. I was young then, much younger than you are now. And it's still the most accurate map of the county."

"Impressive," Simon murmured as it was spread out on the table. Chicken was set aside for the moment as the two men glanced down at the expansive map. He had colored the ridges as well, using dull paints that highlighted the script. Some things had been scratched out and written over, as time made its effect. But as he said, everything appeared in order.

Connelly nodded, and after glancing around for a few moments, he pointed out one section of land, one that had already received a second outline. "Here we are! This is what he thought you might want. A spot close to the ranch and to town, but particularly the train lines. The plot next to them was already taken, but this is the next best option."

Going over his calculations, it looked as though he would have close to ten acres. His family's farm had been twenty, but that's not what he wanted. He did fine on the farm but that wasn't his livelihood. Simon just wanted a little something that would be cozy enough for his family, and comfortable enough through the seasons. Mr. Connelly had mentioned that it had already been checked out for him, handpicked, so Simon knew this would be a good spot. A house, a few animals, a garden, and just a place he could call home again.

"Perfect," Simon grinned at him. "That'll do."

They spent the next hour haggling on prices. Within a minute, he could tell that Mr. Connelly didn't really care about exactly how much money he received, seeing as he would still get some in the end, but it was the art of bargaining that he enjoyed. The men dragged it out until they found something that worked well for both parties. They drew up an agreement that they both signed.

Afterwards, Simon dropped off a copy of the legal sale at the judge's office, and then headed off towards the edge of the town, where a lumberyard was just getting situated in the area. Because if he was going to have a spot of land, then he would need a house made of good timber. Nodding to familiar faces as he went, the young man started on his errands of preparing his future. There was lumber, tools, handy work, and more that he had to set up for.

The sun was setting by the time he completed his errands. Finishing them by purchasing a big bouquet of flowers, Simon considered heading over there that evening to propose to Olivia. Would it upset Susannah, to do it too soon? It felt like forever since he had seen her, even though it had only been a few days. Looking at the sunset, he wanted to go over there and see his girl immediately. But something told him it was still too late, and he was too tired as it was.

"Friday," he took a deep breath, and grinned as he saw the first star of the night come out. "Next week, then."

Chapter Fifteen

After checking the haberdashery and the general store, Susannah retraced her steps and asked the shop owners about Olivia. Each one of the folks she spoke with had confirmed that Olivia had been in and made her purchases. They'd also noted that everything seemed well in order when they spoke with her.

Stepping out of the general store, she looked around anxiously. Her boot tapped against the ground over and over, the only outward sign that she wasn't all right. Well, besides the thick coat and three scarves. She tugged on the top one, groaning as it hampered her view and movement. Her body temperature varied from cold to hot and it was driving her mad.

"Where could she be?" she murmured to herself. What could have taken her off task? Why, even the cart was still there with the horse and their items. Shuffling down the steps, she went to Lemondrop and patted his nose. "Did you see where she went? Hmm?"

She glanced around at the various stores, wondering if she might have wandered into one of them. Olivia always had so much on her mind, but usually she didn't stray from her path. Susannah knew there was only one way to find out, however, so she started off. Sniffling and pulling her coat tight for warmth, she headed into each of the buildings one by one.

And one by one, they couldn't help her. Half of them didn't know who she was, and the others only knew her from a few occasions at church. By the time Susannah had made it halfway around the block, she was tired and sweaty and her nerves were at their end.

Inhaling deeply, she looked around wildly and found herself near the cells. Her heart skipped a beat. Lucas! He'd be able to help. Trying not to shiver from the cold, Susannah bustled her way over to the office. Strength zapped, the wind made her teary-eyed and she could hardly see as she entered the room.

Turning to the desk, she squinted and instantly recognized her husband hunched over the desk. "Lucas!" She gasped, and hurried over. "Lucas! There you are. I've been looking all over. You need to help me—"

He caught her from turning towards the door, grabbing her shoulders. Towering over her, Lucas wiped the tears on her face and she could see his concerned frown. "Susie? What are you doing here in town? Sit down. How did you get here?" And he lifted her off her feet into his chair before she knew what was happening.

If anything, it only made her dizzy. Or dizzier, she wasn't certain. Clutching Lucas with one hand, she blinked several times and waited for the world to slow down to a crawl. She was fairly certain she'd stopped moving, but her head hadn't make up its mind. "Oh."

"You're sick, Susannah, how did you even get here?

You're warm. Too warm." His hands brushed against her cheeks. Wiping his hands on his pants, he glanced around and picked up his scarf, returning to wrap it firmly around her.

Her wide gaze narrowed at him as it covered everything below her eyelashes. No sensible person wore three scarves, no matter how cold it was. She huffed and then sneezed hard several times. "Please, Lucas. Settle down. I needed to come to you. I've been here for hours, I swear, and I don't know what else to do. I've tried everything, and I've looked everywhere."

"But you have everything you need, don't you?" Lucas rubbed her shaking hands. "Where did your mittens go?"

The room was brightly lit and it was still midday, but everything was in a fog for Susannah. Now that she was actually sitting down, her body made a point of reminding her how tired and achy she really was. Groaning, she could feel her bones giving up their strength and she slouched in the seat, grateful for the warmth Lucas was helping return to her bones. But he'd asked her a question.

Her mittens. "My mittens, I lost my mittens! The mittens, oh." He raised an eyebrow and reached into her pocket and pulled them out. Inhaling sharply, her muddled mind told her all was well, until she recalled why she was here. "Wait!" Scrambling up, Susannah tried to pull him towards the door. "We need to find her."

"Her?"

She nodded, wondering why he wasn't budging. "Yes, that's right. Olivia! She came to town with you and she did the things she came to do. I mean, she took care of the errands. Olivia bought what we needed. It's all in the cart!"

"Oh, right." He turned towards the door and away from Susannah.

She ran forward, stumbling over her long coat, and opened the door. Her bones trembled, and she could feel the tingle at the back of her neck that she couldn't ignore.

"I can't find her anywhere, Lucas, anywhere. She's gone! Olivia did everything, but I can't find her." Susannah turned back to her husband, hoping he understood exactly what she was saying. The severity of the situation, she tried not to think about anything terrible that might have happened. Shaking her head, she tried to convince herself if they would just look again, she would be there. Susannah was certain of it. And the more she talked, the louder her voice grew. "She's just gone, Lucas. Without a word. I don't know what to do, but we have to find her."

That's when her husband went over to her, again, but he didn't lead her out the door. Instead, Lucas wrapped his thick arms around her, and she found herself pressed against his chest. "You're shivering, and you're upset, Susie." He stated this as a fact. "You need to take a deep breath, please."

"But—" She couldn't help but obey and gasp for breath. "But I don't know where she went."

"Shh, darling," he murmured, carefully leading her back to the room. They sat on his desk as she collected herself. Now that she had a moment to compose herself, she realized she'd been near hysterics and he had good reason for making sure she collected her emotions before going out in public.

Swallowing, Susannah took another deep breath, and then nodded. She couldn't expect to be of any use if she wasn't collected. "Thank you. But Lucas, we can't sit here all day. Please, I'm worried about Olivia. I don't know where she is. We must find her."

"Neither do I." He paused, looking away. "But I know where I sent her."

"Sent her?" Jerking away, she stared at him. "What's that supposed to mean?"

He pulled her closer before Susannah had a chance to turn away, but she froze at the sound of his heavy sigh. It wasn't just a tired one, it was the one he made when it came to his job. She heard it in the mornings before addressing a hard case in court and in the evenings after a hard day. But what did it have to do with Olivia?

Out of his back pocket, Lucas brought out a crumpled piece of paper. "I received a packet of these to hang around town. Understand, Susannah, that I have no choice when it comes to something like this."

Sniffling, she stared at the sketch and tried to understand the words written below. Surely the fever had taken its toll on her. It seemed incomprehensible, even as he started to explain what was going on, in the best terms that he could explain it to her. But even Lucas lacked the finer details.

"But this is madness." She shook her head, turning up to him. Trying to clear her mind, Susannah took a deep breath. "Her first letter, I should have known it was more serious, but I never would have believed she was hiding something like this. She couldn't hurt anyone, Lucas, I know it."

"I know," he reminded her. "I know. We just need to give it some time. We'll sort this out. I've already sent out telegrams and letters to everyone I know."

"Promise?" She scowled at him.

Lucas nodded. "Of course. I'm sure she'll be back in no time."

Her heart thudded in her chest and she held the paper anxiously. Inhaling deeply, Susannah nodded and forced herself to accept this. Olivia was innocent, there was a mix up. She believed what Olivia had told her husband, and prayed that this would all work out for the better.

"Good. Because she's going to get married and Simon is waiting for her."

Chapter Sixteen

The town of Berryville was nearly the same size as Rocky Ridge, but with a complicated street pattern that left Olivia Foster more confused the moment she made a turn. Upon her arrival, she immediately lost her way and couldn't have left the town if she wanted to. Praying in gratitude for clear skies, she also asked for help and guidance in finding the right place.

What was it that Lucas had said to her? She felt the clink of coins he had given her in her pocket, and she wrapped her cloak tighter around her body. It was still cold in the middle of spring, and all she wanted was a cup of cider and a warm bed.

Something behind her fell, and she jumped at the noise of the loud crash. Clutching her heart, she looked around wildly, waiting to see something she dreaded. Or someone. Her eyes caught the sight of the three men arguing over the broken boxes and spilled vegetables, but she knew none of them. And the more she looked around, the more she noticed how little she did recognize.

Tension spread through her shoulders and she could feel the fear making its way back into the corner of her life. It had started to fade over the last couple of weeks, but returned after seeing the poster Mr. Jessup showed her. Olivia took a deep breath and glancing around knew she needed to start moving. Pulling her bonnet back on properly, she ducked her head down and started walking.

It took her two hours to find the hotel. Lucas had mentioned there was only one, and it was behind the stagecoach station, but it turned out that it meant two streets behind the station and two buildings down. The streets curved and changed without order, so she had passed it three times before realizing what it actually was.

Hurrying inside, Olivia sighed as the warmth breached her skin after so long in the cold. It was a small hotel with only a second floor and small set of stairs to the side, but the carpet was bright and the man behind the desk was cheerful.

"Good afternoon!" He repeated, beckoning her over. "Come in from the cold. How can we help you today?"

With a hesitant smile, she reached into her pocket and held onto the coins. "I'd like a room, please? Just for a couple of days. I'm here to visit with a friend," she added after a moment. "She just had a baby, so I'll be here a few days. We haven't decided how long."

Stroking his goatee, the man nodded and glanced around. "Of course, of course. It's springtime after all, that's when all the babes decide to be born. Now then, let's get you that room. We have a spare on the second floor, first door on your left. Here's the key. Now, might I get your name?"

"O—Ophelia," she stammered, turning red. "Ophelia James." It was the first alternative name she could think of, but it didn't make her embarrassment any less. Fortunately, the man never knew either way. After she paid, he handed over her key and she hurried up to her room.

There were no bags to put away, and Olivia didn't know what else to do once she locked the door and sat on the bed. There was a small chest, a nightstand, and the bed. She had no windows, and nothing else there. Slipping off her shoes, she found herself with nothing to do and all she had with her were her thoughts.

After holding them back all day, now there was no place for them to go and there were too many. The first tear slipped free, and it broke the dam within her. Her heart pounded in her chest and a hiccup escaped. She sniffled, and the rest of her tears spilled forth. Curling up, Olivia picked up the pillow and let the emotions slide over her.

Fear racked her body and she was grateful she was alone, grateful there were no windows for her to be seen. What if they did? What if the wanted signs were hung in this town as well? What if they were everywhere? Or worse, what if Jack's family came after her? Inhaling deeply, she closed her eyes tightly.

Though Lucas meant well, there was only so much that he could do and he had practically told her that she shouldn't return to Rocky Ridge. Olivia tried to figure out exactly where she went wrong, and what she could do about it.

Eventually, it was too much and she exhausted her abilities. Slowly she pulled up the blankets over her body and wiped the tears on her pillow before drifting off to sleep. Tossing and turning through the night, Olivia spent the next few hours cooped up in her room. She ate little, trying to figure out what to do next. But no matter how much she prayed, she couldn't tell if she should move on or stay where she was.

She was wide awake by the time the sun arose. Every part of her was ready to start milking the cows and preparing breakfast but when Olivia sat up, she recalled that she wasn't close enough to the Jessup place to do such a chore. Though it sometimes annoyed her, now she would give anything to be back there.

What if she never went back? The thought had trailed through her mind a few times before, but she hadn't taken it seriously. Now she tried to imagine that. Olivia fixed her dress for the day and pulling on her jacket, went outside for a walk. She had a lot to think through.

It was a cold, blustery day. The sun was out, but the wind cut her skin like knives. Pulling her cloak tighter, she contemplated her options. Glancing around at the town with the brown and white buildings and crowded streets, Olivia wondered how the place could be so disorienting. The streets seemed simple enough, but she knew that the further she went from the hotel, the longer it would take to get back there.

"Well, I definitely won't be staying here," she murmured after taking another wrong turn. Frowning, Olivia glanced around warily, finding a sign for a restaurant. Deciding that she might as well feed herself while she was lost, she went in. She took the first seat she saw and ordered eggs and bacon for breakfast.

When she finished eating, she counted out the money she had left. She figured she could wait here for a week. Then she'd have to do something. If she heard nothing from Lucas Jessup, then she knew she'd have to move on. It was that, she realized, or find herself dragged back to Vermont for trial. Back to Uncle Theodore and Adam Parker.

She shuddered at the thought, dropping her fork. Hurriedly she went up to the counter and paid before stepping outside, hoping the cold air would straighten her up. Olivia braided her strawberry blonde hair, and kept her gaze down as she went.

No matter where she went, she could feel eyes on her, people taking notice of the tall girl with the bright hair that didn't belong there. There was no way to avoid them. Praying there was no one around to recognize her, Olivia hurried back towards the hotel and hoped she would find it more quickly this time around.

Chapter Seventeen

He could hardly sleep the night through with so much energy coursing through his body. Simon tossed and turned, impatiently waiting for the time to pass and the sun to return. It was different this time, however, in the sense that there was energy buzzing throughout his entire body. Every part of him wanted to get up and move, to take action and do something.

It was hard restraining the urge to get up and go see her. It took everything he had to wait, knowing he needed his rest. There was still another day until he was going to propose. Squinting his eyes open to stare at the ceiling, Simon wondered if that meant he really had to wait until then to see her. He would have to endure another tortuous night like this before talking to her.

With the extra time on his hands, he pushed back the rush of guilt and rising doubt. But Lillian was there until it was time for him to head over to the boarding house. After putting on his best suit and preparing his speech again, Simon finally headed out.

His heart hammered all the way there as he pressed

the horse into a gallop. The hoof beats of the horse matched the pounding of his heart, and they worked as one to reach the house as quickly as possible. It was mid-afternoon, and the sun was high in the sky. A slick layer of sweat spread across his forehead as Simon made his way there, leaping off the horse before grabbing the flowers from his saddle bag.

As he reached the porch, Simon briskly fixed his collar and straightened out the wrinkles. Rolling back his shoulders, he took a deep breath and knocked firmly on the door. He pulled on a smile and waited.

"Oh. Simon." Susannah opened the door, eyes wide and half her face hidden in a thick scarf. While she looked much better than when he had seen her last week, the woman was still clearly recovering from her illness.

Perhaps that's why, Simon decided as he nodded at her, she had decided to open the door though they had planned for her to send Olivia to answer it instead. She'd said she didn't want to get in the way of the proposal, and once Olivia answered, they were supposed to go out for a walk. If they returned during suppertime, only then would Susannah intervene, preparing them a picnic under the stars.

"Is Miss Foster here?" He looked around the room trying to hide his confusion.

A mix of expressions spread across Susannah's face. He didn't understand most of them and the few he did recognize, Simon wasn't certain he liked. Shifting his weight, he fussed with his jacket and tried to recall if he was missing anything. He had the flowers, he had polished his boots, his shirt was clean. What else could be the problem?

"Oh dear." She whispered it, and released the heaviest sigh that a small woman could manage. It was more than he would have expected, and it had a lot of weight to rest on her shoulders. "Oh dear, oh dear. Oh Simon."

Susannah Jessup's eyes welled up with tears, alarming him immediately. But before he could open his mouth to ask her what was going on, she grabbed his elbow and pulled him inside. "Um, Mrs. Jessup?" He stammered at the strange action.

"Come in, come in. Please. We need to talk. Lucas? Lucas, where are you? Simon is here. I completely forgot about tonight, and after everything had happened things got out of hand, I suppose. We've been trying so hard to work this out, we've hardly slept. Well, I've had to sleep since I shouldn't have gone to town. I've been in bed all week trying to shake this nasty illness. My point being, Lucas has hardly slept. And I have been desperately worried, I assure you. Waiting on the mail and hunting down information. Lucas went down to Colorado Springs even in the hopes to find more information and it's just been chaos and trouble since."

They entered the kitchen as Simon obediently trailed after Mrs. Jessup but found himself having a hard time following her story. He had no idea what was going on, but from the little he could gather things were not good.

Fortunately, they found Lucas hovering over the kitchen table. It was a beautiful piece of furniture, dark oak that seated eight folks and had engraved designs. Usually it was a lovely sight. But this evening, it was absolutely drowning in paperwork.

Looking up, Mr. Jessup offered an apprehensive nod before raising a hand that stopped his wife's rambling. "She's not here, Simon." The words were simple and short, so short that it took a minute for them to sink in. He walked around the table just as Simon noticed a sketch of a familiar girl, and picked it up. His mouth turned dry as he gaped.

He put the flowers down and stared at the piece of paper, wondering if this was a dream. Heart hammering, Simon tried to imagine Olivia hurting someone but couldn't. So why was she being hunted down like a common criminal? When had this happened? What was going on?

"What happened?"

"She was framed for murder." Lucas started off with that immediately. Simon clung to those words immediately, certain it was the truth no matter what others said. "I've received proof as of this afternoon, Simon. While this is her story to share, I feel there's some parts of it I can give you. The folks back in her hometown wanted to use her, and so she left when she learned of their scheme. That's what brought her here. She was running away from them."

Simon's eyes were wide and his mouth dropped open. He looked in complete shock.

"They bribed an official to send this poster to Colorado towns when they learned where she'd run to from her old boss, Dr. Hadley. But after using my resources, we know they faked this plot and there is no warrant. She's going to be safe."

The tension that had been building in his shoulders didn't dissipate. He started to pace, shaking his head.

It was nearly impossible to imagine, to understand this. "Then where is she? How is she taking this? I need to see her. Why didn't she tell me?" Simon slapped the paper back down, looking back and forth between Susannah and Lucas. "Where is she?" He demanded, louder than he expected.

"I didn't want anyone else looking for her." Lucas put out his hands to calm him down, using his low soothing voice. "I sent her on the first stagecoach out of here."

Susannah grabbed him before he could leave. "Wait, Simon. Please, we had no idea what was going on, and we didn't want her to be in danger." She glanced back at her husband tearfully, clearly overwhelmed. She looked just as he felt in his heart as it beat loudly against his chest. "He sent her on the stagecoach, but we have no idea if she's really there. It's been a week, and she may have gone further, we don't know. We were just trying to decide what to do when you arrived."

He swallowed, and turned towards the hall. "Well, I'll tell you what happens now. I'm going to find her. She needs to know she's safe, and that all this trouble is over. She needs to come back here. Olivia isn't alone anymore. I'm going to make sure of that." He nodded and left without another word, not letting them say anything otherwise.

Back on his horse, Simon turned and rode back towards town. The cold late afternoon air cut across his skin, and every part of him felt alive. His nerves stood on end as he clung to the reins and started off. The evening was coming to a close and the sun had started to set so he raced it west until he reached the next town.

People were still out and about, fortunately. Breathless, he roamed the streets and wound his way through a few blocks before pulling out the sketch of her. Hurriedly he ripped off the *Wanted* script before showing it around, hoping someone might recognize her. Climbing off his horse, Simon asked folks over and over wondering if they had seen the beautiful tall girl with light red hair.

It took twelve people to find one who nodded. "Yes, the woman who eats at the café. She eats there most days." The older woman scratched her thin skin, eyes to the sky. "Doesn't eat much. Doesn't talk much."

Nodding, Simon felt a thrill surge through his veins. "Yes? Where might I find her? Is she still around here?"

She shrugged. "I see her headed in that direction afterwards. Probably the hotel, my dear. You head down that lane, and take two lefts." Her hands gestured limply in that direction, and Simon was off before she ever put her arm down. Zigzagging across the crowds, Simon clutched the sketch in his fist as he finally found the faded hotel sign.

"You have a woman here," he informed the man behind the desk. "Tall. Soft red hair. Big eyes. Quiet. I need to see her."

The man chuckled from his book. "Oh, do you mean our Miss James?"

His heart thudded, staring at the man. Would she do that? Would she call herself that? He tried to imagine a reason, realizing that a woman trying to hide wouldn't use her own name. Of course. But she'd chosen his, of all names. His throat constricted. "Yes. Where is she? Please, I have to see her, I have to talk to her."

"Simon?"

It was only a whisper, but it stilled every bone in his body. Inhaling sharply, he turned and found her there on the stairs, looking right back at him. Their eyes met, and he completely forgot the man he had been talking to. Hurrying over to her side, he took one of her out-stretched hands.

"I've been looking for you." He managed a weak smile.

She sniffed with watery eyes, smiling. "I'm glad you found me."

Chapter Eighteen

The sun was already high in the sky, and it truly felt as though it were already through a good part of the day. It was a lie, however, since it was hardly morning. That's what summer did to people, confused them about the sunlight. Her bones reminded her of the several hours she had already been up, and her stomach rumbled reminding her there hadn't been time to eat yet.

"Ha," she mumbled, and pulled out the right folder. "Here it is. And…oh dear." The pile of letters spilled off her desk. Groaning, she knelt down and still clutching the folder, tried to pull the envelopes and folded papers back into their proper pile. "Of course, it's not like I'm doing anything else right now, am I?"

The door creaked open, and she reminded herself she needed to oil the hinges. Where was that can, in the barn? "Put the letters down." Susannah turned and found her husband standing there with an amused glance down at her. "And the folder."

Standing up, she gave him a sheepish smile and felt

a strand of hair fall out of place. Again. "It's the third time," she mumbled, reluctantly obeying Lucas.

"Then stop running around," he pointed out to her. "It's supposed to a beautiful Saturday, a happy one. And you're ruining it by trying to get everything done at the same time. You haven't even stopped since you woke up. And I know you never slept. Here, eat this." He placed a muffin in her hands and led her out into the hallway.

Perplexed, she stared at the treat. "When did I make these?" Racking her brain, she wondered if it had happened yesterday. There had been a lot of cooking to do. There was the cake, the bread, the pie. But muffins? She sniffed it, uncertain if it was her own recipe.

"You didn't." She looked at him and he smirked. "I did. When you were sorting through the flowers for the third time."

It hurt her brain too much to think about it, so she shrugged and accepted the snack as he led her back towards the kitchen. "This is good," Susannah beamed, offering him a piece that he refused. "You put cinnamon in it, a smart touch. Perhaps I'll take over watching the town and you'll tend to the baking, would you like that?"

Lucas laughed and rubbed her shoulder. "I'm certain that would be quite the experience, darling. But let's consider that tomorrow, shall we? Today, we have busier things to attend to. Like the—"

"The laundry!" She gasped, stopping so quickly that he nearly bumped into her. Both hands fell onto her shoulders as they looked out the window. Her eyes widened, seeing the strong wind nearly pull the linens off the line. "Oh dear. Oh no. Oh, I—"

"Have a wedding to focus on," Lucas steered her away in the other direction. "I'll take them off the line, and we'll take care of it tomorrow. Now, don't you think you should see if Miss Foster is ready yet? You've left her alone for nearly an hour and that's quite unlike you. She may be worried you're ill again."

She shook her head, clearing her mind. "That's right! Olivia. What was I thinking? Today of all days, why would I be so distracted?"

Muttering to herself, she waved Lucas off and hurried towards the young woman's room. She had meant to leave only to put away the linens and find some extra lace. But then she'd noticed another room that needed fresh linens for the next two girls that were headed here from the east, so she'd taken them with her. But after pocketing the lace, Susannah had wondered about their envelopes and began sorting through them to find eligible bachelors around town, so she'd disappeared behind her desk where she'd lost herself in the papers until Lucas caught her.

It was a whirlwind of a day, and it had hardly begun. "I'm sorry." Susannah smiled sheepishly as she returned to the bedroom. "I should have come right back, but my mind has gone everywhere and I don't know what I was thinking, and can't believe I left you alone. How are you faring?"

Olivia beamed at her. "I'm doing quite well, thank you." She picked up her bouquet and it was all wrapped in a lovely yellow ribbon. "What do you think?"

"Beautiful! Almost as beautiful as you are," Susannah chuckled. "Now come here and let me do your hair. Take a seat here, yes. Why, I can't believe it's today. It felt like yesterday when you first arrived. Now I know it's been a few months but the time has flown. Oh, I'm so happy for you and Simon. He is just going to think you're an angel at the church today."

The young woman blushed, glancing down at her dress. It was late summer, so her skirts were thin and light and the dress had short sleeves. It was a pale green, one to match her eyes. It was new and so lovely that she was hesitant to even touch it. Susannah watched her thoughtfully as she braided the bride's hair, twisting it above the nape of her neck. Olivia was quieter than usual, and that was saying something.

"Is everything all right?" Susannah whispered, and touched her shoulder lightly. Holding the brush still in her other hand, she watched the woman's face show the merest glance of concern and dropped her gaze to the floor.

A good minute passed before anything was said. The girl's gaze was indiscernible then, and Susannah forced herself to be patient as she returned to tying up lovely hair. "Everything is perfect," Olivia whispered finally, and met her gaze with a smile. "It's a beautiful day, isn't it?"

Susannah beamed. "It truly is. Now, how does this feel?" She pinned the hair down and stepped back. Clasping her hands together, she tucked them under her chin and considered the young girl. Certainly she hadn't been as pretty as Olivia now on her own wedding day. It had been a quiet affair with just the pastor and Lucas's two deputies at the time as witnesses.

Then, she hadn't even walked down the aisle. On their way to the church, they had plucked a few flowers from the roadside, and Susannah recalled him putting one in her hair and she had smiled at him. The matter had been accomplished in only twenty minutes, and then they'd eaten at the little restaurant in town before going to her new home.

"It looks like you've had a lot of practice," Olivia murmured as she gently touched her hair. "You've been helping a lot of people, haven't you?"

Waving a hand behind her, Susannah shrugged. "Just a few. Now, it's time we were going. Where's your bag? Here it is, good, and you have your flowers." Mumbling to herself, she collected everything that she needed. "I'll be back in just a moment."

"I'll meet you out there," Olivia offered.

Hurrying out, Susannah carried the young woman's bag and started to the kitchen. They still needed to take a few things over for the reception afterwards, and she didn't want to be missing anything. Did they have enough glasses? She wasn't certain. Carrying the bag around, Susannah went and checked everything again.

A box was missing. It was carrying the lemonade, the three glasses she had borrowed for the occasion. But where had they gone now? Tutting, she started looking around the kitchen in case she had mistakenly placed them anywhere else.

"Susie, darling?"

"Lucas!" She jumped and looked at him holding onto the bundle of cloths in his arms. For a moment she had no idea what he was doing until she recalled the laundry flapping in the wind. Sighing, she nodded. "Oh good. I forgot about that. All right. Have you seen the lemonade? I can't find it."

The man rolled his eyes, putting the laundry down and picking up a box. "It's already in the wagon. Along with all the flowers. Lemondrop is ready to go, and he's just waiting on us. Come along now." He led the way out to the wagon where the rest of their items were already gathered. Susannah sighed in relief.

"I'm sorry," she repeated, and found Olivia following behind them. Susannah smiled at them sheepishly. "There's just so much going on. With the girls on their way here, and I met yesterday with another gentleman. With the wedding, then the laundry, my goodness."

"It's fine," Olivia promised her. "I'm sure everything will come off without a hitch."

Lucas laughed, helping the bride into the wagon. "Don't worry, Miss Foster. This is just how she likes to live. It's a terrible day when she doesn't have her hands full." Susannah started to pout but he gave her a wink and squeezed her hand so she couldn't even pretend to be mad. Sighing dramatically, she rolled her eyes as he glanced at them. "Now, are we ready to go to church, ladies?"

The women cheered, and they started off.

Chapter Nineteen

It felt shorter than usual, the ride to the chapel. Clutching the folds of her dress, Olivia looked up and squinted at the sun. Warm and bright, comforting and soothing. Sighing, she leaned back in her seat and tried to relax. Her stomach was a bundle of nerves, filled with butterflies that wouldn't settle down. She couldn't get them out and didn't know what to do about it.

Looking at the puffy clouds drifting above them, she tried to make shapes out of them to distract herself. But all of them kept looking like stars to her, and the stars reminded her of Simon.

The butterflies quieted, and she smiled. Closing her eyes, she thought back to three months ago, when there was still snow on the ground and when she hadn't known where the next day would take her. Being in that little town had given her time to learn to be on her own, only for her to learn that it wasn't what she wanted.

So when she found Simon there, or rather, he found her there, Olivia knew this was Jack's way of letting her go. That this was the right thing to do. And that she really could be safe and happy again. After days of pondering and worrying about where to go and what to do, seeing Simon James had given her the answer.

That day, his soft gaze had melted through her chill and when he touched her hand, Olivia felt something new. After a week of torture by herself, something changed the moment Simon was there. She saw his face light up, and in that moment she was ready to go with him to the ends of the Earth.

"May I talk to you?" He'd asked once he found his voice again, rubbing his thumb across her knuckles. "Please?"

Nodding, she pulled on her bonnet and joined him outside for a stroll. She had just been planning to go out for her supper but thoughts of food went away with him there. Taking a deep breath, she glanced around the area and waited for him to speak.

But when he didn't say anything, doubts began to tumble into her mind. Suddenly she wondered if she was imagining things, that his smile hadn't been what she thought it was. What if she was wrong? Hesitantly she glanced at him and wanted to say something, but didn't know where to start. How did he find her? She didn't know the answer to that.

And why did he find her? Was he glad, like she thought he was, or was it something else? A sense of dread filled her. What if he knew about the arrest warrant? And even worse, if he was here to send her to Vermont? She sucked in a deep breath, trying not to jump to conclusions.

"Why did you come here?" The nerves got to her and she jumped in with the question, stopping in their walk to look at him. Trying to read his face, Olivia bit her lip and waited. Shifting her weight, she tried to pray that her doubts weren't real.

He ruffled his hair and stopped, taking a big breath. He raised his eyes to meet hers and slowly pulled out a crumpled piece of paper. It was the sketch of her, from the sheriff's office. Swallowing hard, she watched as he uncurled the edges. He had ripped off the words, so it looked like it was just a picture, not something criminal.

"There's so much I want to say," he started reluctantly and sighed. Simon stepped back and tried to collect himself. "After we kissed, Olivia, I... I had a lot to think about. Before you, there was someone else. I was married once, if you remember. Before you."

Inhaling, Olivia nodded slowly and looked at the picture in his hands. "Yes. I remember. We both were with someone else once. They were good people—"

"Who we lost," Simon finished for her with a nod. He handed her the picture and took her other hand. "Jane had been with me for all of my life, since we were children. It was only natural that we married when we were older. She was everything to me. But two years ago, she died.

"It was laundry day, but a storm came. I was working with the corn, and never noticed the rising river. I kept meaning to teach her to swim but I thought there was time. It'd never flooded before and she liked the lightning, you know. Jane loved to watch storms." He stopped, his eyes closing.

Her heart hammered in her chest as her own gaze dropped. She knew the pain he was feeling, the agony that felt like it was ripping out your heart and banging against your chest. It felt like everything was on fire and you couldn't do anything about it. As though you were screaming into the abyss and were being torn into a million pieces. Shaking her head, she touched his cheek. "It wasn't your fault."

Simon's eyes opened, wide as they stared back at her. "I always blamed myself," he told her hoarsely. Then he shook his head and looked into her eyes with compassion. "What happened with your betrothed?"

"I lost my Jack." She shrugged with a helpless smile. "And there wasn't anything I could do about it. It was an accident. Sometimes we lose people. I know the pain, Simon. I know it all too well. And thank you for telling me this, but that doesn't answer my question."

Carefully folding the picture back up, Simon tucked it away and glanced at her. "Because telling you means that I've been able to open my heart again. To you, to love." He took the hand that touched his face, and held it in both of his. "Olivia, I know we have this pain, but I've also learned that we can heal from it. And that we can be happy again. I'd like to do that with you, to build a new life and share love again. Would you…is that something you would—um, would you marry me?"

It wasn't what she had expected, she thought, drawing herself back to the present. The wagon stopped and she found herself in front of the chapel. Heart beating, she followed the Jessup couple up through the front doors and found Simon James dressed in his best suit next to the pastor. Olivia's heart pounded as he smiled when their gazes met.

He wasn't Jack, Olivia knew. And he never would be. But that didn't have to be a bad thing. She could feel the warmth burning within her heart, and once again received a confirmation that this was the right choice, that he was the right man that God wanted her to be with.

That day in that little town, she had told Simon James that yes, she would marry him. The answer had burned within her before he even proposed, knowing this was what the Lord had in store for her. After all their pain and suffering, they could find refuge in one another.

Inhaling deeply, she clutched her bouquet tightly as she bustled down the pews and made her way to the men. There was no procession, for she didn't want one. She waved to the familiar faces of several folks from their church on her way down, hoping they weren't too late. The Jessups followed closely after her, taking their place on the first set of benches. They were there to support and represent the family she'd lost. Across from them sat Simon's family, his sister and brother-in-law with their two children.

She paused to wave at the little boy and girl, beaming as they pouted to be dressed in their Sunday best and not on a Sunday. In the last couple of months while she was engaged to Simon, she had met Lillian and often been to the family ranch. The children were energetic and sweet, eager for any sort of adventure. Already they'd made her promise to take them berry picking soon. Upon noticing her, the two straightened up in their seats and waved as she reached the stand.

Simon put out a hand for her, helping her up the two steps. She accepted his warm grip gladly, and found her heart beating a little faster when he didn't let go. Together they stood before the pastor who was grinning at them, holding his Bible. Olivia took a deep breath, realizing she had never been able to go this far with Jack.

But Simon was there, and he was her today and her tomorrow. She squeezed his hand, shyly shooting him a glance as the pastor started talking. He was smiling, and for a moment their eyes met. All eyes were on them, she knew, and half the town was there. But they hardly mattered in a place like this, and especially not now. The only thing that mattered was her Simon.

Chapter Twenty

It was a good house, well-built of good strong lumber and big windows. There were flowers everywhere, and there was a fresh rhubarb pie somewhere nearby. Simon's heart thumped as he reached the porch and found his pace speeding up. For a long time, he had dreaded the journey home from working with the trains, but now he was so distracted that he could hardly focus at work.

Biting his tongue, Simon quietly stepped through the front door, and set his toolbox down. Not wanting to startle her, he slipped off his shoes, pulled off his jacket, and rubbed his face hoping there wasn't any oil on there. Softly he walked down the hall to the kitchen, where he could hear her humming.

"You're my little star, yes you are. My little star in the sky. You're my little star, and how I love to see you shine. Hmm hm hmmm…"

Just watching her there, it eased all the stress in his shoulders and back. He forgot about the blisters and the smell of iron and rust, seeing his Olivia singing as she sprinkled sugar on that delicious rhubarb pie. It was a lullaby, one her mother and her grandmother had sung to her as a child.

It was remarkable how he came to appreciate his wife more every day. After everything they'd been through, their relationship had only grown stronger. Once she returned to Rocky Ridge and to the Jessup place, Lucas had ensured through his own resources that the men trying to ruin her good name were dealt with by the law. The corrupt lawman and Uncle Theodore Henderson had been arrested and would deal with justice in the correct manner, leaving Olivia free and innocent as before.

After that, they had simply needed to wait for him to build their house. Trains usually worked well with fewer issues during the summer so he was needed less at the offices and on the tracks, thus allowing him more time to build. Lucas, Frank, and Jeb were often right there with him, setting up the logs and sanding down the wood until the small house was completed.

He remembered their wedding day only three months before, how happy and shy they were with one another. Leading up to the wedding, he had worried constantly that he would end up comparing her constantly with Jane, but when he saw her in the church in that pretty green dress that made her eyes sparkle, he knew with a surety that it wasn't something he needed to worry about. He would love Olivia for being Olivia.

Finally, Simon couldn't just stand there any longer. "And how you shine, my little star, up so high." And he reached her as she turned around in surprise. He saw her eyes widen before spilling her lips into a bright smile.

"Simon." She stopped, but he had already wrapped his arms around her waist. "You surprised me. It's like you're starting to enjoy scaring me, is that what it is?" Chuckling, she let him twirl her around before licking her fingers with the sugar.

He kissed her cheek from behind, tasting the sweetness that she'd not yet cleaned off her face. She smiled, leaning back with a sigh. "I just like to watch you," he replied finally. "Especially when you sing that. How was your day?"

She nodded, and gestured to the pie. "I didn't find as many berries as I hoped, but it was enough. It's late in the season, but I'm adamant that I'll find a full bush just waiting to be plucked. I'm not crazy, am I?" she asked after a moment.

Stepping away, Simon handed her a cloth to wash her hands. "Of course not. Why would you ask such a thing?"

Flushing, she shrugged. "I don't know. I keep forgetting things. I made it halfway up the hill before realizing I didn't even have my pail with me. And yesterday I never put on my shoes. Honestly, it's not exactly what I was expecting," Olivia explained. "But Susannah and Eleanor stopped by, and they said it was normal."

He raised an eyebrow. "You women never cease to amaze me." She winked and he chuckled. "And how is our little one today?"

Beaming, Olivia pressed her hands against her stomach, still flat because it was so early. She was tall and lithe, graceful as the wind, but soon she wouldn't be able to hide the fact that she was with child. "Very good. Our babe is very, very good. Oh, I can't wait to just hold him in my arms. Or her," she added quickly. "I'll be happy either way."

Pulling her over to the table, he nodded. "As would I. Now rest for a bit, would you? I don't want you tiring yourself out." She gave him a look but did so all the same. Except when he moved to go, she pulled him back with a hand. "Yes?"

"It doesn't mean you should be tiring yourself out either," she reminded him. "Come sit with me for a minute. Besides, you have something on your face. Come here." When he leaned forward, she rubbed across his chin with her warm hand. "There we go. How were the trains today?"

He shrugged. "A few tracks needed to be reset, and I spent some time with the officials since they're considering putting down another path. It wouldn't be for a few years, but they'd like me to head up the project."

She beamed at him, clutching his hand. "That's wonderful! Simon, I'm so proud of you. You'll do such a wonderful job. Where are the tracks leading this time? Will it take a long time? How far are you going to need to travel, or can you stay here? Do you think—"

"Whoa," he chuckled, shaking his head. "Even I don't have all the answers. But all in good time, all right? We can focus on one thing at a time. Like that pie," he pointed out. "And tomorrow, we're going to supper with the Jessups. I passed Lucas on my way back here."

A thought crossed her mind as she turned to the pie. "Perhaps we should save that, then."

His stomach rumbled. "Definitely not," he disagreed. "I think it's just asking to be eaten. Now, right now, actually. I'm pretty certain of that."

"Oh really?" She raised her eyebrow. "I'm not so convinced."

"I wonder how I might fix that." He pretended to think about it, rubbing his chin thoughtfully and staring up at the ceiling. After a moment, he turned back to Olivia who was eyeing him warily, and she didn't move fast enough to escape a kiss. Grasping her chin, he pressed their lips together and caught her by surprise.

Why would anyone want to hurt this innocent woman? Simon thanked God and his lucky stars once again that he was with her and that she'd not run farther away.

But those people in her past could touch her no more, he reminded himself. There would be no nonsense of being sold into marriage or anything else. On their ride back to Rocky Ridge, Olivia had hesitantly shared the additional details of her past, of how good Jack was but how his family clearly struggled to do the right thing. She held little bitterness against them, and it was a lesson to him on kindness and forgiveness, one that he hadn't known he had needed.

After all, he'd blamed himself for over two years for what had happened to Jane. There'd been so many mornings when he woke up with the stabbing pain of realizing she wasn't coming back, and then the ache in the evenings that he hadn't been able to protect her in the end. Yet Olivia was there for him through his struggles, in coming to terms with forgiving himself and no longer placing the blame on him, or anyone else.

She truly was a miracle, Simon decided.

She smiled against him, pulling him closer. Simon sat on the edge of his seat, kissing her until Olivia gave way to giggles, and finally moved back. "All right," she agreed. "I suppose I can make another pie tomorrow, then." She wrinkled her nose at him. "You have such a way of convincing me. Come on, then. I'll let you cut it, shall I?"

Simon took the knife and hovered above the pie just as he looked out the window. That's when he paused at the sight of the two trees recently planted beside the garden. One was a small aspen, swaying in the breeze. The second was an apple tree, young but already full of blossoms. On their wedding day, after the ceremony and reception, the couple had come to their new home and planted those two trees for those they had lost. A sweet reminder of their past.

"Simon?" Olivia brought him back and he turned to her. "Are you all right?"

He nodded, and smiled at her. Her hair was messy and she looked tired, but his wife was glowing and she was clearly happy. Simon could have never imagined that he would be standing there today, but he was. And he was a better man for it.

"I'm wonderful, my love. Truly, undeniably wonderful."

* * * * *